FURY OF SHADOWS

COREENE CALLAHAN

OLIVER
HEBER
BOOKS

EDGE OF SHADOWS

COREENE CALLAHAN

1

EDINBURGH, SCOTLAND – PRESENT DAY

The scent of blood thickened the night air, mixing with soupy fog along rain-soaked streets, carrying the stink along the cobbled length of the Royal Mile. Hidden inside a cloaking spell, Cyprus scanned the deserted avenue from his roof top perch. No dead bodies littering refuse-lined alleyways. Nary an unconscious human in slight. Or even a hint of a blood trail to follow.

At least, not yet.

There would be, though. The stench said all that needed saying. It was only a matter of time before he found the crime scene...and got a bird's-eye view of the carnage.

With a shrug, he resettled his wings and, shuffling left, peered over the parapet. His night vision sparked. His eyes started to glow. A pale purple wash rolled out in front of him, coating all it touched, allowing him to see in the dark as he searched dense shadows. Dragon senses dialed to maximum, he fine-tuned his sonar. A pedestrian turned onto High Street. The thud of foot-falls rang through the quiet. One eye on the male, the other on the city skyline, Cyprus watched the unsus-pecting human jog up a set of shallow steps and, keys jingling, let himself in to a flat fronting one of the busiest thoroughfares in Edinburgh.

A total tourist trap.

People from all over the world came to walk the Royal Mile and visit the Castle on the cliff. View the magnificence. Touch a piece of history. And be regaled by bloody battles and the brave Scots warriors who'd fought in each.

Cyprus glanced south. Pretty place, Edinburgh Castle. Lit by bright lights, thick stone walls glowed like a beacon in the dark, inciting creative imaginings, setting the stage for yet another long night. He shook his head and, dragging his focus from the fortress, stifled a growl of frustration. What a fucking mess. His mission should've been easier than this—than being forced to cool his heels while the rogue male he hunted played hide and seek in a busy human city.

Clenching his teeth, he shifted sideways and rounded another corner, his eyes trained on the ground below. The tips of his claws scraped the low wall as he moved. Nothing. Still no sign of the bastard...or the dead bodies.

Annoyance made his muscles tense. Combating his impatience, he rolled his shoulders. Iridescent black scales reacted to the shift, ruffling into a cascade of clickety-click-click. The jagged spikes along his spine joined the parade, clattering in the quiet. A whisper of disquiet rattled through him. The situation stank of a set-up. A well-devised trap with one purpose in mind—to draw him away from Aberdeen, into a city he didn't know well and liked even less.

"And so, the hunter becomes the hunted." Winter chill fogged his exhale, making white puffs rise in rings above his nostrils. "Clever."

Or so the bastard believed.

The rogue, though, had failed to take crucial point into account. Cyprus never engaged in anything random. He plotted and planned instead. Which explained why he'd made the trip south now, didn't it? The instant he sensed the strange male fly into his territory, he'd chosen to do what his enemy wanted—played the fool, allowed himself to be lead and followed the breadcrumbs. To what end? His mouth curved. For the hell of it. For the need to avoid layering one boring night atop another. For the sheer want of a good, claw-ripping fight.

Crouched like a cat, he leapt to the adjacent building top. The yawn of an alley flashed beneath him. His bladed tail whiplashed. The click of his scales sliced through the cold as the wind picked up, rustling the trees standing sentry over vacant sidewalks. He landed with a thump and walked along the edge, attention on the street below, the rasp of his paws against tarred roof tiles loud in the stillness.

The cacophony of sound didn't matter. Nor did it travel. He made sure of it with a murmured command, strengthening the shield of invisibility that concealed his presence from human and Dragonkind alike. Eyes narrowed, irritation rising, he looked over the raised roof edge and scanned intersecting alleyways. For what seemed like the thousandth time.

"Come out, come out wherever you are." His upper lip curled, exposing the twin rows his serrated teeth. "I want tae play."

His voice hissed through his fangs, the invitation hanging in frosty air. The acceptance he craved didn't come back. Silence reigned instead. Cyprus flexed one of his front talons. Bloody hell. The bastard was smart. Or scared shitless. One or the other, but...no way to tell until he set eyes on the warrior who'd invaded his

territory. The bold move worried him. All of Dragonkind knew to stay clear of Scotland. The land, sky,
mountains and lakes—shite, all of it, every nook and
cranny, down to the last blade of grass—belonged to
his pack, and no one crossed his border without suffering the consequences.

Immediate death by dragon claw.

He liked the sound of it. Wanted to follow through
on the promise, but with the rogue using city streets to
hide, he couldn't smoke him out without doing serious damage. The thought didn't bother him—much.
Humans, after all, thrived on misery. For whatever reason, their race enjoyed demolition and reconstruction,
so...aye. He could level an entire city block, turn it to
rubble, create new jobs, fuel their economy with one
tiny fireball. Inhale. Exhale. Crash, bang, slam. Simple. Nothing to it as long as he didn't take human lives
in the process. Big satisfaction. No guilt. The perfect
crime.

Cyprus snorted at the thought. Fire-acid sparked
from his nostrils, heating the air as he jumped to another rooftop and—

"Anything?"

The inquiry thumped on his mental door. Cyprus
linked in, accepting the connection with his first in
command. *"Not yet."*

Wallaig growled. *"Is the wanker really going to make
us hunt all night?"*

"Looks like it."

"Christ," Wallaig said, pure annoyance in the soft
curse. *"Of all the nights to be away from the lair, this isnae
one of them."*

The comment made him pause mid-stride.
Cyprus's brows snapped together. *"Why?"*

"Rannock's making Haggis for breakfast. I want to be home when—"

A gagging sound came through mind-speak. *"Fucking disgusting. I hate Haggis."*

"Shut yer yap, Levin," Wallaig snapped, his irritation redirected from the hunt to his pack-mate. *"Donnae you dare insult his cooking. If you hurt his feelings, he'll stop making—"*

"One can only hope," Levin said. *"That shite smells like vomit and—"*

"Tastes even worse," Kruger murmured, finishing his best friend's sentence.

"Aye, well, think what you like, but..." Wallaig trailed off, waited a few seconds, the threat of violence shimmering in the silence. *"If you ruin the best meal I've had in weeks, I'll make sure you suck yer next one through a straw."*

"You'd have to catch me first, old man."

"Whelp," Wallaig said, his voice so deep he sounded past homicidal and well into satanic. Cyprus knew better. Could detect his first in command's enjoyment in every vicious syllable. Wallaig might be the eldest of their pack, but he loved a good fight—verbal or otherwise. *"I'm going to rip yer claws out and nail yer scrawny arse to the ground with them."*

Levin snorted.

Cyprus grinned. The threat wasn't a new one. Wallaig promised to de-claw one of them at least once a week. Hell, the pledge of violence was practically the male's way of saying "I love you". Shaking his head, he ignored the continued banter of his warriors—and Wallaig's vow to gut Levin like a toad and feed him is own entrails—and refocused his search. Over by the church, mayhap. The scent of blood grew stronger the closer he came to St. Giles Cathedral—to sacred ground held by priests and forgotten prophets.

His attention shifted to the crown-shaped spire atop the church. Surrounded by golden light, the High Kirk of Edinburgh glowed, pouring light onto cobblestone streets and the square butted against its front entrance. With a growl, Cyprus leapt from one building to the next, his gaze fixed on the stone walls of the cathedral. Blown by a brisk wind, the acrid smell of spilled blood spiked. He snarled, the savage sound shredding the air in front of him. Bloody hell. Could the bastard really be that depraved? Had he taken the fight to humans on holy ground?

The question circled less than a second before—

Shock made him freeze where he'd landed.

Gaze riveted to the square, Cyprus sucked a horrified breath. One second ticked into two before the true extent of the carnage registered. Goddess help him. Dead humans lay everywhere. Decapitated and de-limbed, body parts strewn from the base of the statue in the middle of the quad to the church's front steps. Like a sick kind of bread trail. Or the beginnings of a grotesque human puzzle with too many pieces to fathom. He didn't want to count, but...shite. There had to be at least five—mayhap six—different humans in the mess.

"*Mother of God,*" he whispered. "*The bastard.*"

Wallaig paused mid-insult. "*Cyprus?*"

"*What's going on?*" Kruger asked, the intensity of his focus so keen Cyprus registered it from three miles away. "*What do you see?*"

"*Dead humans...everywhere,*" he said, voice gone hoarse. "*Or at least, what's left of them.*"

"*What the fuck?*" Levin growled.

The click of scales echoed inside his head.

"We're on our way."

"Nay, Wallaig. Stay put."

His first in command cursed.

Cyprus growled a warning and, gaze glued to the human casualties, leapt over the roof edge. The rush of cold air curled over his horns. Six feet from the ground, he transformed, shifting from dragon to human form. Dropping fast, he conjured his clothes. Jeans, a T-shirt and his favorite leather jacket wrapped him in warm comfort as his booted feet landed on stone. Rising from his crouch, he looked both ways, searching the empty street for humans. Nothing so far. Only one conclusion to draw—no one had stumbled upon the massacre yet. Which meant he needed to move...and it had to be now. Before someone came along and called the police, forcing him to leave.

"Hold your positions, but be ready tae move." He didn't want to spook his enemy. The second his warriors took flight the rogue would sense the power of his pack and run for his life. Cowards always did when faced with superior strength, so...nay. Better to keep things under wraps until he got his claws on the male. Stepping off the sidewalk, Cyprus crossed the street. "I'm going tae take a closer look."

"Jesus Christ," Wallaig grumbled, not liking his plan. Or the fact he waited outside the three-mile maker—distance enough to avoid being detected by the enemy, too far away to be of any help if the situation devolved and shite hit the proverbial fan. "Watch yer arse, laddie."

"Is the rogue gone?" Kruger cracked his knuckles, the sharp snap echoing through mind-speak.

Cyprus shook his head even though no one could see him. "He's still here...somewhere. I smell him. I think he may be in the church."

In fact, he was sure of it.

He scented the bastard now. Plain as day. No need to question his dragon half. The scent trail grew more intense with every step he took. And as he stepped into the square and strode past the statue of a long-dead Duke—stepping over amputated arms and legs, skirting heads with jagged neck wounds and mutilated human torsos, boot soles splashing through puddles of human blood—the senselessness of it slammed through him. Rage burned a hole in his heart, waking the vicious urge to annihilate everything his path.

His dragon half seethed, wanting out of its cage.

Cyprus obliged, letting the killer inside him out to play as he reached the front steps of St. Giles Cathedral. He took the stairs three at a time. How dare the bastard murder innocent people in his territory. He might not like the human race, but those who lived inside his borders did so under his protection... whether they knew it or not. So aye. Retribution now belonged to him. Their deaths must be avenged and a clear message sent. No one infringed on his land. The rogue had just signed his own death warrant. All he needed to do now was find the male and complete the kill.

2

Feet beating a furious pace on the sidewalk, Elise Woodward skidded across uneven pavers in front of the five-story walk-up. The instant she stopped sliding, she grabbed the handle and flung the front door wide. Ancient hinges groaned a warning. Beveled glass rattled in the pitted wooden frame. She ignored the clatter and, heaving her shoulder bag, raced across the lobby. Without looking, she shot past the elevator with a stained *Out of Order* sign taped across its face, and made for the stairs. Her shoes rapped over cracked floor tiles. The strike of each footfall echoed, buffeted by a low ceiling in the small space. Her heart adopted the rhythm, hammering inside her chest as she took the steps two at a time.

Out of breath, palm slapping against the handrail, she rounded the next landing and headed for the fifth floor. Almost there. Another thirty seconds, and she'd be home. Keys in hand and at her apartment door. After that, she had...Elise glanced at her watch and grimaced. Crap. Less than five minutes to change her clothes, grab her kit, and dash into the night again.

Otherwise, she'd be late.

For her very first consultation.

That it happened to be with a priest was neither here nor there. Late was *late*, no matter how God fearing or forgiving the client.

Worn carpet bunching beneath her heels, she stopped in front of her apartment door. Pea green paint peeled from the surface, revealing different colored layers underneath, the same way a Gobstopper did when cracked open. Digging her keys out of her bag, Elise drew a deep breath. As she exhaled, she shoved her key in the lock. The metal teeth stuck, resisting the forward momentum. In a battle with the deadbolt, Elise shook her head. Yes, indeedy. She lived in a real peach of a place, so low-brow even the paint protested, curling away from the door, obscuring part of the number seventeen screwed into its center.

With a hard twist, she turned the lock, cranked the handle and—

"About time you got home." Graced by a thick French Canadian accent, the voice came at her like an arrow from the kitchen tucked into the back corner of the flat. Elise glanced in that direction. A pastry chef at a popular downtown bakery, Amantha stood like a pixie armed with baking prowess. All of five foot nothing and stationed at the butcher block that served as the kitchen island, her best friend—and roommate—wore a red apron with pink piping and a threat on the front—*How can you help? GET OUT OF MY KITCHEN!*

Reading the warning, Elise closed the door and raised a brow. "Not going well?"

"Stupid soufflé. It collapsed when I took it out of the oven." Her friend scowled at the pan sitting on the cooling rack next to her.

Her lips twitched.

Amantha's eyes narrowed. "You laugh, you die."

She held up both hands in surrender.

Dark brown eyes leveled on her, her friend plunked a turquoise mixing bowl down on the countertop. Brandishing a pink-tipped whisk like a sword, Amantha pointed at the clock hanging between two arched windows in the living room. "You're late, El. You're never going to make it if—"

"I know. I know." Lifting her bag over her shoulder, Elise flung it toward the loveseat. The leather satchel bounced, assaulting frayed purple upholstery as she skirted the bistro table and jogged toward the short hallway to the right of the kitchen. Wrestling with the buttons on her coat, she swept past the narrow refrigerator, turned into her bedroom, and kicked off her shoes. "I got caught up at work."

"On a book?" Hot on her heels, bright green spatula now in hand, Amantha appeared in the open doorway. "Or is Attila the Nun breathing down your neck again?"

Elise swallowed a snort of laughter. *Attila the Nun?* Really? As curator of the rare book and paper conservation department in the National Museum of Scotland, her boss might be exacting—obsessive even—but honestly, Dr. Scott wasn't all bad. Although...she frowned... Amantha might be on to something with the whole *nun* thing. In the six months Elise had worked at the Museum, her boss hadn't gone out once. Not on a single date. Hell, the woman spent so much time in the conservation laboratory, Elise couldn't be sure she ever went home at all.

Or owned real estate outside the rare book library.

"A new exhibit arrived today," she said, tossing a tank top onto the twin bed pressed against the back wall of her tiny room. "I unpacked all the boxes to make sure nothing was damaged during transport."

"Well, you've got..." A furrow between her brows, Amantha plucked her phone from her apron pocket. Striped peppermints cartwheeling across the back of her phone case, she glanced at the screen. "Three minutes to change and get out of here. Father Matthew might lock up if you're not there at ten, like you promised."

Stripped down to her underwear, Elise wiggled into her designer jeans. Even on sale, she'd spent too much money on the pair, but well...hell. She hadn't been able to walk past without grabbing them. Elise smiled as she zipped up. So flattering. Super comfortable. Dark denim, perfect for every occasion. Just right for a relaxed meeting with a new client.

God, she hoped it worked out.

She wanted the job. The extra income would be nice, sure, but getting the nod from Father Matthew—and her hands on the antique book collection in St. Giles's library—meant more than the money. She needed the reference for her resume. A letter of recommendation from the priest would help her land the only fulltime job available in the Book Conservation Department at the Museum. As it stood now, she was one of four interns vying for the position. With her degree in Applied Museum Studies—and a concentration in book conservation—she had a shot. But with less than a year's experience? She flexed her hands. Less time on the job meant less employable. Elise sighed. The way of the world sucked sometimes.

So did the threat of going home.

Elise blanched at the thought.

Not that she didn't like Ottawa. It was a nice city, the place she'd grown up, but...ugh. The idea of returning home with her tail tucked between her legs—of proving her father right—rankled. She was independent now. Much better off on her own. She'd fought too hard, for too long, to crawl out from beneath her Dad's overly critical thumb. No way would she give up her dream of one day becoming the rare book curator in the National Museum of Scotland.

Not for her father. And certainty not for Gus Whittaker...the overbearing asshat.

With a scowl, Elise reached for her favorite V-neck sweater. The magenta cashmere caught on the coil of her low bun before slipping over her head. *Gus.* Elise crinkled her nose. What kind of a name of was that anyway? A wimpy one. An annoying one. One without an ounce of integrity, just like the man. God. Thinking about the cocky jerk made her want to reach for one of the battle axes in the medieval exhibit.

Gus actually believed he was a shoe-in for the job. He was so sure the head curator would select him for the position, he never stayed late or helped other interns. Not that she wanted him anywhere near her, but well...

Adjusting her sleeves, Elise smoothed the cashmere cuffs. Gus and his arrogance bugged the hell out of her. The rat-faced fink needed his ego smacked down and his butt kicked...and not in that order either.

Elise paused to look up at the ceiling, imploring the God of Payback to descend on Rat-faced Whittaker and deliver what he deserved as she looped a scarf around her neck. "I hope you're listening."

Amantha rolled her eyes. "Superstitious much?"

"Just a little," she said, shrugging. "Never hurts to ask."

"Well, do it with your feet moving." Amantha pointed at her with the end of her iPhone. "Get going."

"Yup." Slipping into her boots, Elise shoved her

arms into her coat and, adjusting the collar, brushed past her friend on the way to the front door. "I'll call you when I'm done."

"Good and—oh merde. I almost forgot. Hang on a sec."

Halfway across the living room, Elise glanced over her shoulder. "What?"

Grabbing a brown paper bag off the top of the fridge, Amantha tossed it to her. "For Father Matthew."

The bag crinkled as she caught it. "Muffins?"

"Cranberry-apricot. Fresh from the oven." A sparkle in her dark eyes, Amantha winked at her. "His favorite."

Gratitude punched through to grip her heart. God love her best friend. No one knew better than Amantha what impressing Father Matthew meant to her. Meeting her friend's gaze, Elise smiled. "You're all kinds of awesome."

"You know it," she said, grinning from ear-to-ear. "Now, shoo and...bon chance!"

"Luck's got nothing to do with it," she said, holding up the bag. "I'm armed with muffins. He doesn't stand a chance."

Amantha laughed.

With a wave, Elise snagged her satchel off the couch, tucked the muffins inside, then grabbed the briefcase housing the tools she used to repair rare books. Please Lord, give her the opportunity to use it. That's all she needed, a chance to show the priest her skills and convince him the church's library needed someone like her to see to its care. But as she exited the apartment and jogged down the stairs—hard plastic kit banging against the outside of her thigh— doubt poked at her. What if Father Matthew said no?

What if he refused to grant her access to the manuscripts in need of repair? What if her plan fell apart, and she didn't get the reference she needed to impress the panel of Museum curators deciding who got the job?

The questions tightened her throat.

Elise shook her head. No sense worrying about it now. Negativity never got a girl anywhere. She'd made a decision and set her course. Had told Father Matthew she would be there, so...onward and upward. Time to put some skin in the game. The priest was expecting her. Which meant she needed to up the pace. She had a fifteen-minute walk ahead of her, just enough time to reach St. Giles Cathedral, slip through the side door as promised, and meet her soon-to-be client.

3

S ilent as dead humans in a crypt, Cyprus cracked the heavy door open and slipped into the cathedral. A rush of warm air greeted him, brushing the night chill from his skin. The smell of old stone and fresh incense swirled as he stopped inside the vestibule. Conjuring a spell, he gathered the gloom, shadowing his form and, without moving, glanced around. He grimaced. A church. The rogue must be warped—or worse...brilliant—to lead him inside a human holy place.

Shifting further into shadows, he absorbed his surroundings. Solid wall in front of him. Two points of entry—one on his left, another to his right. Instinct turned him toward the double archway. Boot soles skimming over huge granite pavers, he crossed the threshold and mounted a set of shallow steps. Magic throbbed through the quiet, ghosting like invisible fingers across the floor to grab at his ankles. His dragon half stirred, sharpening his senses as he hunted for the rogue's unique energy signal inside ancient stone walls.

He needed to locate the bastard. Now. Before he fled...

Or killed anyone else.

Muscles tense, ready to fight, Cyprus veered into the side aisle. Rows of thick pillars reached for the vaulted roof as one soaring arch flowed into the next. Fine-tuning his sonar, he surveyed the cavernous space. Nothing yet. No sign of the enemy, but...he swallowed a growl. Had he mentioned how much he hated human churches? The architecture was always so bloody ornate: too many columns, deep alcoves and fancy altarpieces, not enough open spaces. The building was a nightmare to navigate, providing the enemy with multiple points of escape.

Inhaling through his nose, he filtered the scents, allowing his magic to mine dark corners. He cast his net wide, then gathered the threads and pulled. Intel rose up lobster traps being pulled from the ocean floor. His sonar pinged. The sharp sound echoed inside his head. An answering blip came back and—

Energy whiplashed.

An image of a male formed inside his mind. Right there...playing hide and seek near the front of the church.

His mouth curved. "Gotcha, you bastard."

Footsteps light, Cyprus moved fast, using the towering pillars for cover as he ran beneath gilded chandeliers and past spectacular stained-glass windows. Reaching the nave, he glanced to his right. Back pressed to the east wall, an organ stood tall, immense silver pipes rising in the gloom. It was a nice piece. Pretty in many ways, magnificent in others. Probably sounded gorgeous when played and—

Cyprus shook his head. No time for daydreaming. Or being tempted by the promise of music. Any other night, he would've given in to the urge. Sat down. Let his fingers walk and the piano keys talk. But not

tonight. Now needed to be about the rogue using humans for target practice, not his love of all things
musical.

Hitting his haunches beside a wooden pew, he
took a moment to scout the enemy's positon. A
scraping sound ricocheted off the stone walls. His
focus snapped toward the cloth-covered altar at the
front of the cathedral.

A thump echoed.

Cyprus's eyes narrowed. Shite. Not good. The thud
sounded a lot like a fist meeting flesh. Or a body hitting the ground.

Swallowing a curse, he spun around the nearest
column. Pinned to the top of the pillar, a vertical flag
fluttered, reacting to his velocity as he pivoted into the
center aisle. Stone dust kicked up. The pungent smell
of incense grew stronger. A vicious crack vibrated
through the church. Clenching his teeth, Cyprus entered the nave and—

He saw the downed priest first.

On his back, sightless eyes turned toward a set of
stained glass windows, the Father lay face-up in front
of the main alter. Rising from his crouch, Cyprus
dragged his gaze from the human and stepped into the
open. No sense checking on the male. Or calling an
ambulance. The priest was already dead, his skull
cracked, blood pool spreading as his limbs twitched
and gray matter oozed onto the stone floor.

Turning his head, Cyprus focused on a row of
chairs behind the altar. A faint shimmer disrupted the
darkness, helping him pinpoint the rogue trying to
hide inside a cloaking spell. Rage simmered through
his veins, igniting aggression and his need to maim.
He shut down the inclination, refusing to move too
soon.

Patience was a virtue for a reason. Avenging the priest's murder would happen—eventually. A few more minutes of letting the rogue live wouldn't hurt. It could, however, help him understand what the hell was going on. Something was up. *Something* big for the male to enter his territory and kill his people...right under his nose. So aye. He needed to know why first and save the violence for second.

Circling right, he left the priest where he lay and stepped farther into the nave. The shimmer expanded, then contracted. Cyprus stared at the male who believed himself undetectable. "Planning tae hide all night?"

A huff echoed through the quiet. An instant later, the rogue uncloaked. Tall with a lean build and shaved head, the bastard smiled, highlighting the blood splatter on his cheek. "About time you caught up with me, pretender. Slowing down in your old age?"

Delivered in a Danish accent, Cyprus let the insults roll right off him. No sense reacting to the idiot. The comments, though, caught his attention. One reference to his age, which meant the rogue considered younger better. A misconception, but...whatever. Let the bastard believe whatever the fuck he wanted. What interested him was the *pretender* accusation. What the hell did that mean? As the question banged around inside his head, the past came roaring back. Cyprus tensed as unease pulsed through him. What did the rogue know? Had he unearthed the secret he'd kept for over fifty years—from his blood brothers, from his pack-mates, from the Dragonkind world at large?

The idea tightened his chest.

Cyprus breathed through the physical lockdown,

refusing to flinch. Or lower his guard. No way would
he hand the rogue an advantage. Not here. Not now.
Never, in point of fact.

Stalking forward, he herded the rogue toward the
side aisle. "Want to tell me why you're killing
humans?"

The rogue shrugged. "Why not? It's good sport.
Humans make the most interesting noises when
cornered."

Good sport. Disgust rolled through him. The arsehole needed his head ripped off. Cyprus bared his
teeth. "What the fuck are you doing in my territory?"

"Is it really, pretender?" Red irises rimmed by gold
met his. An odd sense of familiarity chimed through
him as the Dane raised a brow. Cyprus frowned.
Something about the male tweaked his antenna.
Seemed familiar somehow and—an image flashed
through his mind. Bloody hell, after all these years
and...shite. The resemblance couldn't be denied. In
the right light, the bastard looked too much like a warrior he'd once known. "Or did you steal this land from
your sire? And mine too?"

"Who are you?"

"Grizgunn...son of Randor, first in command to
your sire."

"I know who your bastard Da was," Cyprus said,
voice so low it registered as a snarl. Goddamn it. Just
as he feared, his past sins front and center, on display
before God in the middle of a human church. Aggression churned through him. Now he ached to do what
he'd done all those years ago—put Grizgunn down
the same way he eliminated own his sire. "I hope he's
dead. Nothing but a pile of ash in a shite-hole of a
place."

"Asshole." Temper showing, Grizgunn flexed his

hands and stepped around the last chair, challenging him from ten feet away. "You are not the rightful commander of the Scottish pack. You stole the title the night you murdered your sire. My father was next in line...to be crowned pack leader before you maimed and chased him from the island."

"Bullshite."

Well, mostly. Grizgunn wasn't wrong about his culpability.

Cyprus was responsible for his father's death. He'd ended his life, executing his sire for a crime so heinous he knew his Da had gone insane. No other explanation existed. Not then. Not now. As much as it killed him to admit, his sire had lost touch with reality and fallen in with the Archguard, orchestrating the ambush and murder of his uncle—commander of the Scottish pack at the time—and cousins, Droztan, Conn and Forge...young males in their prime and his best friends.

The knowledge still pained him. Left an open wound on his heart and a mark on his soul. Time hadn't help. Knowing he'd done the right thing didn't either. He still longed for his uncle's leadership and missed his cousins, carrying the guilt of not realizing what his sire planned until too late.

If only he'd listened to his instincts.

Cyprus had suspected something was wrong with his sire. He'd watched the slow unraveling of his mind for months, but hadn't understood what it meant. Or how dangerous the secret meetings with Rodin— leader of the Archguard—had become. A strong male, his uncle had chosen a direction for the Scottish pack and stood in Rodin's way, rallying other pack commanders, opposing the male's bid to become High Chancellor of Dragonkind.

Hindsight. Cyprus clenched his teeth. What they said was true: it was twenty-twenty. Now more than ever.

If he'd known then what he knew now, he would have done things differently. Brought his sire to stand trial. Exposed the conspiracy concocted by Randor and allowed the pack to decide both warrior's fates... along with the method of execution. But he hadn't done that. In his outrage and grief, Cyprus had taken it upon himself to right the wrong. Instead of involving his blood brothers and pack-mates, he chased his sire down. Randor had been in his sights as well. The male had gotten away, slipping through his claws before he delivered the final death blow.

Now, the past reared its ugly head.

Grizgunn appeared to be the face of it.

One he wanted to punch a hole through. Hitting the bastard would feel fantastic. Killing him would be even better.

He could have ignored the challenge to his leadership—forgotten about the past and welcomed home a lost member of his pack—if not for the dead bodies outside. The murders, however, sealed Grizgunn's fate. A warrior who preyed on humans would never be welcome in his territory.

With a snarl, Cyprus fired up mind-speak. *"Wallaig —get airborne."*

"St. Giles?"

"Aye. I'm nose-tae-nose with the bastard." Gaze locked on his target, Cyprus pivoted, each stride a calculation, forcing Grizgunn to react. He stepped around the dead priest. The Dane walked backward, keeping equal distance between them. Smart. Good for Grizgunn, 'cause aye, the second he got his hands on the male, he'd snap his neck. Quick and clean. Brutal with

the benefit of a high crunch factor. Merciful too, more than Grizgunn had offered the human priest. *"Surround the church. As soon as I make a move, he's going tae run and—"*

"On our way." Scales rattling, Levin took flight. *"Distract him. Keep him talking long enough for us to lock down the area...close all avenues of escape."*

"Will do," he murmured, keeping the link with his warriors open. The flap of multiple wings echoed inside his head. He closed the gap, forcing the Dane to keep pace. "Any last words, Grizgunn? Make it quick. I've run out of patience."

Pipe organ looming at his back, Grizgunn sneered. "Bastard Scot. You think you're so smart."

"Is that right?" he asked, just to be contrary. Well that, and to anger the arsehole glaring at him. Chitchatting with the Dane might not be pleasant, but it served a purpose. The angrier Grizgunn became, the less attention he would pay to the pack flying in to surround him. "Tell me, whelp...what else do you know about me?"

Grizgunn's nostrils flared. His red-gold gaze started to glow. "My sire—"

"Was a traitor. His scheming lead tae the death of my kin."

Grizgunn sneered at him.

Raising his fists in blatant challenge, Cyprus growled back, daring the bastard to—

The door to the side entrance flew open. Light from the street poured into the cathedral, cutting a swathe across the tile floor. "Father Matthew?"

Female voice. The clatter of shoe heels echoing on stone. "Sorry I'm late, but..."

Stunned by the sound of her, Cyprus listened to her lovely voice fade. Horror struck as the mystery woman came into view. Head bowed, arms pumping, she rushed up the stairs. White hot energy blurred the air around her, making her aura glow in the dark. Heat hit him like a battering ram. Hunger merged with desire. Cyprus jolted as magic cracked like a whip, lashing his skin, addling his mind, gluing his feet to the floor.

Grizgunn fared no better.

Shocked by the rare sight of a high-energy female, the Dane gaped at her.

Propelled by primal instinct, Cyprus stepped forward, her bio-energy a lure he couldn't resist. Jesus help him. An HE...here, in Edinburgh, standing less than twenty feet away. One with no idea who stood inside the church. Not the priest she called for, but two hungry Dragonkind males feuding over territory and—

Her foot connected with the last step. Her wee chin rose, presenting him with the prettiest face and bluest eyes he'd ever seen.

"High-energy." Awe in his expression, Grizgunn rounded on her.

"Go back, lass!" Shite. He was too far away. No way would he reach her in time. Grizgunn stood closer, a handful of strides to his twenty feet. Cyprus waved his arms to warn her. "Get out!"

Blue eyes wide with confusion, she stopped. Her gaze tracked to him, then landed on the priest. "Oh my God—Father Matthew!" She dropped the briefcase she carried. As hard plastic hit the floor, she ignored his warning and ran forward. "Call an ambulance!"

Desperate to reach her first, Cyprus lunged to intercept.

Grizgunn moved faster. Shifting behind her, the Dane grabbed a fistful of her hair. He yanked. With a yelp, the female jerked to a stop. Her feet left the floor. Cyprus tried to intervene, shifting right then left, desperate to close the gap, but—no chance of intercepting now. Grizgunn already had her by the throat. She was locked down. Caught in cruel hands. Trapped by a warrior who enjoyed inflicting pain and making humans suffer.

4

I n full flail, Elise grappled with the man grabbing her from behind. One hand around her throat, the other fisted in her hair, he yanked her backward. Her feet left the floor. Shock buffeted her, ripping her from reality as the asshole dragged her toward the side door of the church. She reached over her head, hands curled like claws. Her nails scratched over forearms protected by heavy leather.

He laughed.

She screeched and tried again, swiping at his face. He hauled her upright, putting her on her toes. Hot breath rushed against her ear. Panic gave way to fear. Her thoughts splintered, echoing the chaotic bang of her boots on the stone floor.

Her heart joined the parade, thumping hard against her breastbone. She sucked in a breath, trying to think. She needed to *think*. Figure out how to break his grip and get away, but...dear God, what was happening? A second ago, she'd been fine—on time, goal in mind, the promise of victory in her grasp. Now, she fought a guy she couldn't see, never mind stop. He was too big. So very strong. No matter how hard she struggled, she continued to lose ground.

Bucking against his hold, she yelled in fury.

Her attacker twisted his fingers in her hair. Pain ripped across her scalp. "Quiet, female."

"Screw you," she rasped, seeing spots as he squeezed her windpipe. Almost out of air, she punched backward. Her knuckles struck something solid. His head jerked to one side. Agony exploded across her hand. Clenching her teeth, Elise ignored the pain. Good. Finally. A direct hit. "Get off me! Get off!"

Letting her arm fly, she elbowed him in the ribs and lunged sideways. With a grunt, he lost his balance. She launched another attack. Her hand snapped toward his face.

"Fuck." The asshole ducked.

Her fist sailed wide, grazing his cheekbone.

Teeth bared on a snarl, he shook her like a can of soda. Her brain fizzed. She saw double for a second, but refused to stop fighting. One good shot. A quick knee to the balls. A hard stomp to the top of his foot. Her thumb digging into his eye socket. That's all she needed...*one good shot*. If she got lucky, if she caused him enough pain, he'd let her go.

Drawing her knee up, Elise kicked backward. Her boot heel slammed into his shin. He growled in warning. Terror lending her strength, she flailed, determined to break free.

"Be still—or I'll snap your neck." He hissed the threat in her ear, wrapping her tighter against him.

His chest bumped against her back, making her stomach pitch. Bile burned the back of her throat and—oh God. She was going to be sick all over herself. Tears pricked the corners of her eyes. Gritting her teeth, she refused to let one fall. No way would she cry. She would fight. Channel every bit of her energy into hurting him more than he was her.

Making twin claws, Elise raked her nails across his face, leaving bloody tracks on his cheek. She tried to gouge him again. With a growl, he dipped his head. His teeth found an exposed patch of her skin. He bit down hard, slicing into muscle. Pain blurred her vision. A hot river of blood rolled over her collarbone. She gasped. He increased the pressure, cut deeper, ripping at her shoulder. The excruciating burn spread, numbing her arm, making her cry out, the faint rasp more sob than shout.

Fingernails digging into her throat, he withdrew his teeth from her skin.

She whimpered.

He hummed. "Nice. Squawk some more, female. I like the sounds you make."

The threat should have made her comply. She should go limp, cease struggling—do something... anything...to ensure the pain stopped. The enjoyment she heard in her captor's voice wouldn't allow it. She couldn't let him win. The second he dragged her out the church and into the street, her chances of survival diminished....by a factor of a million. Every self-defense class she'd taken said so, the message always the same—never let the attacker take you to a secondary location, no matter—

"Grizgunn!" The deep voice rang against the high ceiling. Elise flinched. Her attacker froze and, raising his head, stared at someone across the church. "Hurt her again, and I'll—"

"What, pretender—what will you do?" Grizgunn nipped the wound on her shoulder. As she winced, he growled in her ear. "I hold all the cards, every advantage...along with her."

"So you think."

"So I know," Grizgunn said, yanking on her hair.

Agony spiked, streaming down her spine.

The second man cursed.

Elise gritted her teeth, smothering a gasp of pain. No way. Not going to happen. She refused to provide the asshole with more of the sounds he enjoyed hearing. She'd die—or put him in a shallow grave—first.

Grizgunn dragged her toward the exit.

"Jesus. Easy. Go easy," the other man said, the rage in his voice unmistakable. "She's high-energy—too valuable tae damage. There's no need tae harm her."

Faint footfalls whispered through the cathedral.

"Stay where you are, Cyprus," Grizgunn said. "One more step, and I gut her."

She heard a rustle. More footsteps. The soft shuffle of someone approaching.

Immobilized by a punishing grip, she looked through her lashes. The owner of the baritone tinged with a Scottish accent stepped into view and...God. *Him*. She remembered now—the sight of him as she entered the cathedral. How she could have forgotten about him, Elise didn't know. The guy was hard to miss, never mind ignore.

Taller, broader, more muscular than her attacker, Cyprus struck her as invincible. The angular planes of his face backed up her theory, giving him a predatory air she appreciated given her situation. Grizgunn was wary of him, maybe even afraid. She heard the disquiet in his tone, read the tension in his body and the nervous jerk of his hands.

And no wonder.

Grizgunn's fear made perfect sense.

Everything about Cyprus screamed dangerous: the way he moved, the resolve in his expression, the in-

tense way he assessed Grizgunn, searching for weak-
nesses, looking for an opportunity to strike. He wasn't
fooling around, which meant, neither could she. She
might not know him, but as Cyprus walked closer,
forcing Grizgunn to retreat, instinct aligned with her
impression of him.

He was safe. Somehow, she knew...*he was safe*.

Elise reached for him, stretching out her hand.
"Help me."

Pale violet eyes flicked to her. His gaze met and
held hers. A shock of recognition pulsed through her.
Absurd, perhaps, but something about him settled
her, calmed her, rang true in ways she didn't understand and refused to question. Logic ceased to exist.
Her reaction to Cyprus—the trust she placed in him
without good reason—didn't need to make sense. Not
here. Not right now. He wanted to free her. She
needed the rescue, so...

"Cyprus," she whispered, a plea in her voice.
"Please—help."

"I will, lass, but donnae struggle." He maintained
eye contact a moment more, helping her breathe,
holding her steady, then returned his attention to
Grizgunn. "Stay as still as can be, *talmina*. Cooperate,
and he willnae tighten his hold."

Cooperate? Go willingly? The advice gave her a bad
case of the shakes. But as her teeth started to chatter,
Elise ceded to his suggestion...even though, she hated
the idea. Going down without a fight didn't feel right.
The man holding her hostage would hurt again. The
nasty bite on her shoulder—the painful grip of his
hands, the brutal press of his body—left little open to
interpretation. Every instinct she owned told her to
struggle. She wanted to claw Grizgunn's eyes out, but
she couldn't fault Cyprus's reasoning. He was right.

The more she resisted, the rougher Grizgunn became.

Tears welled in her eyes. "Don't let him take me. Please, don't let him—"

"Look at me, *talmina*," Cyprus said, soft reassurance in his tone. "Whatever happens, keep your eyes on me. Glued tae me—aye?"

Fixing her gaze on him, Elise tried to nod.

Grizgunn tightened his grip, delivering more pain. "Touching. Are you this soft with all your females, pretender?"

Nostrils flared, Cyprus circled left, testing Grizgunn's limits. "One chance—I'll give you *one chance* tae save your own hide. Let her go and leave, whelp. Live tae fight another day."

"Go fuck yourself," Grizgunn said with a hiss. "The female is mine—the spoils of war. Back off...or watch her die."

Reaching the top step, Grizgunn dragged her down the stairs. Her feet scrambled over the stone treads. Fear spun her around the edge of insanity. Her focus on Cyprus, she begged him with her eyes—her body, her expression...everything...anything, just as long as he didn't leave her. She wouldn't survive Grizgunn. Cyprus knew it, and so did she. The asshole might let her live...for a little while, long enough for him to play cat to her mouse: inflict maximum damage, make her scream and suffer, watch her bleed some more. But in the end, he'd become bored with the game and find someone new to prey upon. Sadists always did. Which meant...

She was as good as dead if Cyprus failed to free her.

"Cyprus," she said, clinging to the sight of him like a lifeline.

His eyes started to glow. A purple shimmer made her breath catch as Cyprus met her gaze. An odd sinking sensation took hold. The world dropped away, making her lose her bearings. Unmoored, Elise whispered his name again. A buzz erupted between her temples. The gentle burn pierced through her fear, blurring her vision as something foreign materialized inside her mind.

She blinked, a slow up and down.

A voice whispered, *"Hold tight, lass. Help is almost here."*

Thick Scottish accent. Undeniable command in his tone. Cyprus's voice, his words, but...how was she hearing him? He hadn't opened his mouth. His lips hadn't moved, and yet, she knew he spoke to her. Elise frowned. Odd, but it felt as though Cyprus was inside her head. Then again, maybe there was a better explanation. Maybe, she'd just lost her mind. Misplaced like it like an airline did luggage the second Grizgunn grabbed her. Anyone would have, given the circumstances: crazy sadist and weird glowing eyes notwithstanding.

His eyes began to glow brighter. The voice came again. *"Remember,* talmina—*whatever happens, eyes on me."*

"Whatever happens," she said, repeating the command, 'cause, well...hell. If she was going to accuse herself of insanity, she might as well go all the way and act like a mental case as well. "Okay."

"Good lass."

Breaking eye contact, he flexed his hands. Inferno-like heat slithered through the church. The air warped and went murky. Light bulbs flickered, the hiss of electricity crackling in warning. Grizgunn cursed. Cyprus shouted, his battle cry a call to arms. Orange flame rose around him, racing over his shoulders as he charged forward, his glowing gaze on her.

"Wallaig—now!"

His roar jolted through her.

Wind howled through the cathedral. Fire raged into an inferno, engulfing the walls. As the blaze collided with the vaulted ceiling, a hard crack exploded through the nave. The side door shattered. Wood splintered. Shrapnel nicked her cheek as Grizgunn howled in pain. Hard hands still at her throat, she felt him move behind her. He became bigger, rougher, the fingers around her neck growing into claws. The sharp tips scraped her skin as she hit her knees and looked up. Elise sucked in a breath, then lost it again. God, no, it couldn't be. Just wasn't possible, but...holy shit—the asshole had grown into a dragon with blue scales, razor-sharp claws, and jagged black horns on its head. Red eyes aglow, the beast snatched at her with a huge talon.

Her butt hit the floor.

"Get up, lass!" Flames billowing around him, Cyprus sprinted toward her. "Run!"

Excellent advice. Too bad she didn't take it.

Frozen in place, she stared at the nightmare rising above her. Shock sank her ability to think. Incredulity did the rest, seizing her muscles, stealing her breathe, making her a stationary target.

The beast took advantage of her momentary lapse.

Monstrous claws flexing, it plucked her off the floor, caging her in its giant paw. Hard scales grazed her skin. Panic slammed through her. Her heart rampaged, pumping her full of adrenaline. The jolt rebooted her brain. But it was too late. The instant her mind came back on line, the dragon unfolded its wings. With a powerful thrust, Grizgunn blasted through the church roof, rocketing into the night sky before she gathered the strength to scream.

5

Galvanized by the female's fear, Cyprus sprinted across the cathedral. His heart beat double time. His ability to sense her shot forward, hanging onto to her like grabbing hooks and...thank Jesus. He could still feel her. Was connected in the most elemental of ways: embedded inside her thoughts, locked inside her mind, experiencing her kidnapping first hand. He gritted his teeth and ran faster. Goddess forgive him for not reaching her in time. Terrified. She was absolutely *terrified*, crying out his name, reaching for him through the spread of razor-sharp claws as Grizgunn turned tail and fled.

The bastard slashed at the ceiling, widening the gap.

Slate tiles poured through the jagged hole, shattering against the church floor. His dragon half snarled. His magic flared. Orange flame followed, licking over his shoulders, making his chest heave and knees piston. Footfalls echoing against stone, he watched Grizgunn escape into open air.

Bloody hell. Not good. The bastard held the ad-

vantage now—was ahead of him, in dragon form...
with the female clutched in his talon.

Legs and arms pumping, Cyprus inhaled. His
lungs expanded. Fire and acid pooled, combining into
a nasty cocktail at the back of his throat. A single exhale, and he'd fry the bastard. Take him apart scale by
scale as his particular-brand-of-brutal scorched the
webbing on Grizgunn's wings. The perfect plan, but
for one problem. He couldn't unleash hell. Not with a
female in the middle of the target zone. The second
the force of his exhale stuck, toxic liquid would splash
up and out. She'd be burned alive, the fury of his fire-
acid incinerating her on contact.

With a growl, Cyprus sucked in more air. The shot
of oxygen hit him like rocket-fuel. Speed arrived like
an explosion, thrusting him forward as Grizgunn's
spiked tail disappeared from view. The female
screamed again. The fear-filled cry resonated inside
his skull and—

Goddamn it. He was a dumbass.

No way should he have allowed the male to shift.
Pinning him down in human form would've been better. The best strategy, advisable all the way around,
but well...shite. He hadn't counted on *her*: the sight of
her, the scent of her, the zip of her energy fogging the
air...along with his brain.

He'd never encountered anyone like her. Not once
in all his years of living. Like an inferno, the female
burned bright, possessing the kind of bio-energy
Dragonkind males yearned to touch. Sad to say, he
was no different. He'd played the fool the moment he
laid eyes on her: imagining, salivating, hesitating just
long enough to give Grizgunn the upper hand.

Goddamn it. He was an idiot.

He never should have entered her mind and

spoken to her. The psychic touch—the brief reassurance—had been a mistake. A distraction he couldn't afford. He'd known it the moment she opened her mental doors and invited him in, accepting his presence...making his heart thump, his mind throb, and his dragon drift left of center.

Not a great idea in a fire fight, but...to hell with it. Forget about Grizgunn. His priorities had shifted, dampening his need to annihilate, giving him a new mission...the female. All he wanted—all he could think about—was retrieving her. Taking her home. Ensuring her safety while he saw to her comfort.

Catapulting off the top step, he leapt skyward and shifted into dragon form. Black and white scales speckled orange rattled over his body like a fast-moving bush fire. Heat blasted through him. Aggression followed as he unfurled his wings. Orange webbing caught air. With a powerful thrust, he spiraled through the hole in the ceiling. His view of a stormy sky expanded. Night vision sparking, he flew around the church spire and—

"Cyprus—right flank!"

Levin's voice. A fireball flashed in his periphery.

Cyprus somersaulted into a sideways flip. Green flame streaked past, singeing his wing. Pain pulsed over his shoulder. Cyprus ignored the discomfort. Fucking Grizgunn. Was the bastard actually challenging him in open skies? Shite, he hoped so. The whelp wouldn't stand a chance. Not against him. Bigger, stronger, more experienced than Grizgunn, he'd descale the male faster than it took to peel an orange.

A lovely plan. One problem with it.

Grizgunn wasn't stupid. The bastard had brought reinforcements. Eight males strong, the contingent attacked his warriors. In a bright burst of red scales,

Wallaig feigned left and banked right, nailing two rogues with his claws on the fly-by. Cyprus grinned and scanned the battle as Kruger attacked a rogue head-on and Levin grabbed another by the tail. With a snarl, his warrior dragged the male backwards through the air. Wing-flapping, the rogue shrieked. Levin growled and, whirling around, slammed the turquoise-scaled idiot skull-first into the side of a building.

Brick crumbled into the street below.

The scent of dragon blood filled the air.

The sky broke open. Rain fell as lightning flashed across the night sky.

Raindrops peppered him, then slid along his scales. Cyprus barely noticed. Busy hunting for Grizgunn's blue scales in the storm glow, he increased his wing-speed and watched Wallaig gut a male. A violent north wind blew in. He scanned the horizon beyond the city, searching for the female's unique energy signal, trying to see through smoke and rain. She had to be here, in the fray...somewhere. Grizgunn wasn't that skilled. No way had he found a way around the fight so fast.

More lightning cracked overhead.

Another dragon roared.

Panic set in. Bloody hell. He couldn't hear her anymore. The tether connecting him to her kept stretching. Was thinning by the second. Hunting for her, he circled away from the protection of his own pack. *"Where the fuck is he?"*

"Who?" Green, black-tipped scales flashing, Kruger latched onto a rogue. Triple bladed claws sank into the male's neck as Kruger drove him backwards. The rogue screamed in pain. Without mercy, his warrior twisted. Bone snapped. The brutal crack echoed, and

the male disintegrated, coating Kruger's scales with ash. *"The idiot inside the church?"*

"Grizgunn," he said. *"He has a female."*

"For Christ's sake." Speed supersonic, navy, gray and gold scales slick with rain, Levin chased down another rogue. *"Why didn't you hammer the arsehole inside?"*

Cyprus bared his fangs on a snarl. *"The bastard had her by the throat."*

"Ah," Wallaig said with something close to sympathy. Cyprus cringed. God save him from his own warrior. The older male surpassed eerie on the rising intuitive scale. Wallaig never guessed...at anything. He didn't need to. His XO read males like open books, unearthing the truth without ever asking a question. *"She's yer mate."*

Bull's-eye. Dead center. Wallaig was in fine form tonight. *"I donnae know. Not for sure."*

"You didn't get close enough to touch her?" Grabbing a rogue by the hind-leg, his XO turned and threw him at Levin. As Levin murmured "thank ye" and punched the male in the face, Wallaig flew in behind him. *"Well —what say you, lad?"*

"She accepted me. I spoke to her, Wallaig."

"Through mind speak?"

"Aye and...goddamn it—I cannae see shite from here." Angling his wings, Cyprus rocketed into a tight turn. A rogue hissed at him on the fly-by. Cyprus pulled up short and lashed out. His claws struck yellow scales. Blood splattered his forearm. Talons digging deep, he held on, cutting through muscle to reach bone. The rogue squawked. Cyprus revolved into a terrain-blurring spin. On the third revolution, he released the warrior. Unable to control the flight, the male slammed face first into the cliff below Edinburgh Castle. *"I need a visual, lads. Now—before Grizgunn gets away."*

"Pale blue scales?" Spiraling into a back flip, Levin sliced through a rogue's wing with his spiked tail. *"I see him."*

"Where?"

"North. The arsehole's using the fight to cover his retreat."

His attention snapped left. Cyprus searched the sky north of the city. The downpour blurred the landscape, but...a glimmer of blue shimmered in the storm flash. *"Got him. I'm—"*

"Go, Cy," Kruger said, hammering another rogue.

"Retrieve her," Levin said, seconding his best friend. *"We've got this."*

Focus locked on Grizgunn, Cyprus disengaged from the fight. He swung north, giving Kruger a wide berth as he took on two rogues at once. *"Follow when you're through."*

"Might be a while," Wallaig said. *"Might have to show the bastards a thing or two. I haven't had this much fun in years."*

Cyprus snorted, then shook his head. Crazy bastard. His XO never backed away from a fight, but to prolong one? He thought about it a moment. Aye. No question at all. Wallaig wasn't above playing with his prey before he killed it.

"Oh, and Cyprus?"

"What?"

"Cover yer arse, laddie." The crack of scales echoed as Wallaig stabbed a rogue with the horn he'd just ripped off the male's head. *"Grab her and go. No heroics without back-up."*

The advice pissed him off.

A bad reaction. Particularly since Wallaig was right.

Hunting alone never amounted to a good idea.

Neither did risking a high-energy female. But as he tracked Grizgunn across the rain-soaked sky, over Forth Bridge and into the forest north of the firth, the urge to ignore the rules jabbed at him. He might be commander of the Scottish pack, but he was a male first and foremost. One with the need to protect a female. Possessiveness ate at him. Territorial instinct pointed the way. He wanted the male dead for hurting her. Nothing less than complete annihilation would satisfy him. Not now. Not ever. One way or the other, back-up or nay, he would see her safe, then make Grizgunn pay for daring to take her at all.

6

The whirl of treetops made Elise's head spin. The bite mark on her shoulder throbbed, making her wish for a return to numbness. No such luck. Cold air burned across her cheeks, tearing at her hair as pain ripped in waves. The agonizing rush spiked along her spine, colliding with the base of her skull. Squeezing her eyes shut, she struggled to breathe: past the pain, past the panic, past the impossible and the realization she was screwed.

Miles above ground. A sadistic dragon in control. No way to escape. Not enough air in her lungs. No Cyprus in sight.

Tears flooded her eyes. Her bottom lip trembled. Elise shook her head. *Breathe. Breathe. Breathe.* The word ran like a printed column inside a college text book. The never-ending scroll turned litany didn't help. Her body might be rebelling, struggling to draw oxygen, but her mind worked just fine. She knew where she was—trapped inside a dragon's paw, razor-edged claws inches from her face. From her chest. From a heart beating too fast to help her think.

With a growl, Grizgunn tightened his grip.

Sharp claws flexed around her. The rip of heavy

fabric rent the air a second before pain burst across her back. Warm rivulets rolled beneath her sweater. Swallowing a sob, she reached around to check. Holes in her peacoat. Blood soaking through the cashmere underneath. She pulled the material away from her skin. The sticky sensation set fire to her temper. Goddamn the asshole. He'd just ruined her favorite sweater, which was...absurd. Such a stupid thought given the situation—and the fact she was about to die.

She wanted to scream in outrage anyway. As ridiculous as it sounded, the ruination of her clothes was more real than the cuts on her skin. She couldn't face the horror of her injuries. Couldn't reach out and grab hold of the truth. Her mind rejected reality, forcing her thoughts away from the inevitability of torture into the idiotic. Elise knew it, but didn't care. She needed the coping mechanism—no matter how farcical—to help her survive a little longer. But as Grizgunn nicked her again, Elise lost control and gave him what he wanted—a whimper of pain.

He laughed, the awful chuckle triumphant.

She contracted into a tighter ball. The flex pressed her knees to her chest as a tear rolled over her cheek, mixing with the rain pelting her through dragon claws. Not knowing what else to do, Elise reached for what she'd sensed inside the church. A lifeline. Cyprus had given her one, helping her stay calm, keeping her fear at bay, feeding her confidence with little more than the sound of his voice. He might not be here now. She might be a breath away from death, but...

She reached for him anyway, seeking solace in the memory. "Cyprus."

"*Here.*" The word, driven by a deep growl, tapped her temples. "*Brace, talmina.*"

She blinked. *Brace? For what?* Had she really heard that or...

Lightning forked overhead.

Raising her head, Elise peered around Grizgunn's talons. Nothing. She couldn't see a—

Grizgunn jerked mid-flight. His horned head whipped around as a black hole opened in the sky behind him. Pale purple eyes flashed inside it, piercing the dark a moment before a flamed lasso shot out of it depths. Rain burned away in a blast of heat. The inferno grabbed Grizgunn by the tail. The loop tightened. The force on the other end of the fiery rope yanked. Grizgunn shrieked as he got dragged backward in mid-air. The violent movement jolted her. Her head whiplashed, slamming her teeth together.

Black spots swam in her vision.

Elise fought stay conscious and, squinting into the gloom, searched the sky. A black dragon with white speckled scales rocketed out of the vortex. Orange wings spread wide, he wound the fire lasso around his fist and yanked again. Grizgunn bucked, trying to sever the leash. The second dragon held firm, reeling Grizgunn in like a fish on the end of a line.

Recognition slammed through her. "Cyprus!"

Huge fangs flashing, he answered with a roar. The ungodly sound ripped at the fabric of sound, making her ears ring and—

Grizgunn panicked.

Monstrous wings flailing, he thrashed, struggling to break free. Fire exploded in a sunburst of flame. The smell of burning flesh permeated the air. She gagged. Cyprus didn't quit. He kept pulling and, claws deployed, slashed at Grizgunn. Scales cracked. An inferno engulfed the tip of Grizgunn's tail. He screamed. Dragon blood flew, hitting her like paint spatter as

Grizgunn whipped around and, holding her over his horned-head, drew his arm back.

"Nay!" Cyprus lost his grip on the lasso.

With a roar, Grizgunn launched her like a baseball.

Stormy sky raging around her, she left his talon and hurtled into open air. Massive treetops sped beneath her. Like jagged teeth, the rocky terrain rose to meet her. Gravity did the rest, dragging her toward the ground. Further away from Cyprus, and a thousand steps closer to death.

7

The instant Grizgunn threw the female, Cyprus opened his talon and let his prey go. His claws scraped over the bastard's scales. The fire lasso disintegrated, snapping its tail as magic whiplashed inside his mind. So unsatisfying. God-damn frustrating. He wanted to make the male to scream some more, but—

He couldn't take his eyes off the woman.

She was everything. The answer to a lifetime of loneliness.

Presumptuous? Probably, but Cyprus didn't care. Prudent or not, he allowed hope free reign and hunted for her instead, seeking the glow of her aura amid dark storm clouds. Rain slashed at him. Thunder boomed, rattling his scales. A second later lightning forked overhead. The bright flash lit up the night sky. He caught a glimpse of her blonde hair.

Tucked in a small ball, wet tendrils whipping around her head, she plummeted, her bio-energy a beacon in the dark. Half hanging onto Grizgunn, he shoved his enemy one way and dove the other. His night vision sparked. He narrowed his field of sight, refusing to lose her in the storm. Thick clouds billowed up and out. She disappeared into the swirl. He lost sight of her again and—gone. She was simply *gone*, falling faster than he could track her.

Concentrating, he fine-tuned his sonar. A ping sounded inside his head and...

She reappeared on his radar.

His eyes narrowed. Shite. Not good. The wind buffeted her, rushing her toward the ground. Panic made him fold his wings and become an arrow, his target the bio-energy she carried like a tracking device. He needed to intercept her while he still held a chance of pulling up. If he didn't, he'd hit the ground right along with her. He rechecked his position. Bloody hell. She was falling too fast, dropping like a stone, shifting in and out of his line of vision.

With a growl, Cyprus spiraled toward the ground. The storm hampered his vision, slowing his speed. Reaching deep, he summoned more magic. Her bio-energy flared in his mind's eye. His scales caught fire, flickering over the spikes along his spine. Inferno-like heat spread. He ignored the light show. The flash'n-fly didn't matter. With his dragon half raging, flames were par for the course. His beast liked the blaze and his body needed the extra magic. Like rocket fuel, it propelled him forward, increasing his velocity, cranking his sonar to maximum levels.

A faint blimp echoed between his temples.

Cyprus snarled in satisfaction as he reacquired his target, locking on to her bio-energy and—there. Right fucking *there*. Directly below him, falling through thick clouds and punishing rain.

Pushing himself to the brink, he raced to intercept her.

Cold air lashed over the horns on his head. A white jet stream whistled from the tip of his bladed

tail. Approaching treetops helped him triangulate.
Her life force burst through the heavy clouds, making
his mind burn and his senses seethe. Hooked onto the
signal, he tracked her without seeing her. The chaotic
beat of her heart battered him, scraping along his already frayed nerve ending. Concern for her gripped
him. She was past panic, well into terror, in danger of
having a heart attack. Another bolt of lightning and...
shite. He was in trouble: off course, too far east of her
position. The howling winds shoved him farther afield
with each new gust.

Frustration combined with fear. Jesus help him.
He was close enough to see her now, but still too far to
catch her before she collided with jagged rocks below,
unless he did something stupid. Something unsafe,
for the second time in one night.

One foray into the magical chasm—when he'd
chased down Grizgunn—his dragon could handle.
Entering into the time-space continuum for a second
time in less than an hour might well kill him, but—
Cyprus bared his fangs—fuck it. He couldn't let her
go. Refused to leave her to the fall and himself to the
merciless twist of fate.

Ignoring the danger, Cyprus aligned with aerody-
namics. A strong updraft hammered him. He called
on his magic. The powerful surge streamed into his
mind. He grabbed hold, looping it over and around
him. Fire swirled into a funnel. Opening his wings, he
banked hard. A loud boom exploded around him.
Heavy clouds disappeared. The wind died and the sky
warped, ripping a wormhole into the fabric of space
and time.

Note wasting a second, Cyprus sliced through the
gateway.

Magic howled a warning. His dragon flinched.

Cyprus ignored the beast. No time to waste. He needed a miracle, and as taut muscles twisted around his bones, he sent a prayer heavenward, beseeching the Goddess of All

Things. He wasn't a weak male. Hell, he was stronger than most, but faced with failure, he didn't know what else to do. Here, right now, he needed *her* help. He didn't deserve it. Wasn't arrogant enough to believe she'd answer his plea, but he prayed she would listen.

"Please," he murmured. "She's mine. I need her."

As if in answer, the pressure inside the vortex increased. Speed went supersonic. Pain pressed down his spine, compressed his rib cage, threatening him with suffocation. Absorbing the agony, he spiraled into darkness flecked with swirling stars. He murmured a thank you to the goddess and honed in on the female's location in the night sky. A gamble. Nothing but a guess, but as the walls inside the corridor flexed, he let his magic unfurl, hunting for her signal in the real world, beyond his position inside the continuum.

The wormhole tunneled in front of him.

As the walls contracted, Cyprus held his breath and braced for impact.

The fire circle reformed.

Sparks blazing from his scales, Cyprus shot back into the here and now. In full tantrum, the storm raged, lashing him with a weather-fueled whip. He sucked in a deep breath and, with a quick flip, reoriented himself in the sky. Where the fuck was he? He blinked to clear his blurry vision and...okay. All right. Good to go. He was in reverse position, his back to the ground, wings still tucked to his sides, clouds above him. Letting himself fall he waited, searching for her.

Please God, let him be in the right position. Let him be—

A soft glow flashed above him.

The powerful pull of her bio-energy slammed through him.

Cyprus growled in triumph. His gamble had paid off. He was right where he needed to be and now, locked on target. Unaware of his presence, she fell toward him. He kept his eyes on her and counted out the seconds. Time to intercept: three, two—

Thunder boomed overhead. Another flash of lightning.

One!

He heard her hitching sob a second before he reached out. The tip of his claw snagged her coattail. He pulled her sideways in mid-air. Fabric ripped, splitting up the seam. She squeaked, flinching as he reeled her in and checked her vitals. Eyes squeezed shut. Bio-energy throbbing. Whole body trembling. Petrified, but still breathing.

"Easy, *talmina*." Pulling her closer, he spread his wings, slowing his flight, and settled her against his chest. "Easy."

"No, no, no-no-no." Still curled in a ball, she shook her head, adding to the denial. "I don't want to die. I don't want to die."

"No one's dying," he murmured, trying to sound human. It didn't work, and no wonder. In dragon form, he sounded like a monster: all hiss, too much fang, little to no reassurance. Suppressing a snarl, he tried again. "Easy, baby. I've got you."

She tucked in tighter, turning her face away from his scales, refusing to open her eyes.

Afraid of him. Too lost inside her own head to see him as her protector. His dragon half howled at the unfairness. Cyprus shut his beast down. The damn thing would just have to wait—for her to calm down, for her to stop whimpering...for her to accept him as her male.

The bond would form.

It had to.

With her in his paws, the connection already bloomed. Like tendrils on an octopus, her bio-energy wrapped around him. He breathed in, drawing on her scent as satisfaction sank deep, soothing him in ways nothing else ever had, and as the hum intensified, gathering strength and speed, Cyprus recognized her what she was—his mate.

The realization tightened his chest.

Tucking away the emotion to draw from later, he rotated in mid-air, flipping upside right. His tail clipped the treetops. Wet bark punched skyward. Ignoring the debris trail, he banked right, whirled around a cliff face, and glanced down at the female in his claws. Shite. She wasn't any better. Still in distress. Beyond frightened. Shivering uncontrollably, even though he used his magic to warm her.

His concern for her swelled.

Cyprus shook his head. As much as he wanted to, he couldn't soothe now. Locked inside her own mind, she wouldn't listen to anything he had to say. He needed to find cover and get her out of the storm first. The faster his paws touched the ground, and he shifted into human form, the better she would relate. And the quicker he'd seen to her injuries.

How badly she was hurt, he didn't know. But he could feel bio-energy fading: the fear, fatigue and blood loss from her injuries taking a toll, making her body weaken.

Increasing his wing speed, Cyprus scanned the

rough terrain, searching for a safe place to land. He flew up over a rise. No...not there. He considering a small clearing, but...no. It wouldn't do either. Too exposed, not enough cover: nowhere to lay her down and touch her skin-to-skin. Only his hands on her would do now. Healing a female always worked best when a warrior took human form.

He wanted to soothe her, but needed her trust. Otherwise, she would fight him, and the bond he required her to accept wouldn't form.

A dangerous thing for her right now.

He didn't control the connection. It all came down to her. She must acknowledge and accept the bond that would permit him to feed her. Forcing her wouldn't work, which left him with just one option— convince her to feed or lose her forever.

8

Everything hurt. Her head. Her muscles. Her skin. Even the marrow in her bones throbbed, making her mind scream and her body shake. Like a series of powerful aftershocks, tremors rumbled through her, rattling her teeth, upping the agony, propelling her into a brutal downward spiral only ER doctors knew how to stop.

Not that she could be fixed.

A bleak thought, but Elise accepted it as she fought to breathe. Oxygen in. Pain out, her chest struggling to rise though each bite of fresh pain. Over and over. Again and again until each exhale sounded pathetic, less wheeze, more whimper, weaker with every breath she took. Treetops sped beneath her. Cold air nipped at her cheeks. Hard scales and sharp claws surrounding her. She tried to struggle, to keep her eyes open and her mind working, but...nope. No hope at all. There wouldn't be any escaping...or fixing her.

The slices across her back told a sickening tale. She was pretty sure one of her kidneys was damaged, cut open by Grizgunn's claws when he tossed her like a baseball. Now, she bled, the slickness under her

sweater turning to sticky ooze and...goddamn the asshole. He'd thrown her away like garbage, as though
she didn't matter, and—

Elise frowned. Something had happened to make
him do that.

Something powerful.

Something important, but...Elise shook her head.
No. That wasn't right. It wasn't a *something*. It had been
someone. Her brows furrowed. Right? Hadn't it been?

She searched her memory, trying to recall what
she'd witnessed. The truth refused to surface. Confusion bubbled up instead, blurring reality. Now, she
couldn't tell fact from fiction. Had any of it been real?

She remembered a ring of fire and the violent
crack of impact. Felt the way Grizgunn jerked in mid-
air, heard his scream inside her head, but...she sucked
in an agonizing breath, struggling to sort through what
she'd seen. Nothing clear formed. Just a scattering of
imagery—thoughts and perceptions—that made no
sense. Scales and serrated teeth. Fire and bite of wind
chill. The pain and mind-torque of mental blur.

Weakness setting in, her head bobbed forward.
Her cheek brushed something warm and hard. A
growl reverberated through the ridged surface. She
pressed closer, soaking up the heat, listening to the
rumble, needing the connection.

Another growl. More skin-stroking vibrations.

The pain eased a little. Just enough to push her toward numbness.

Elise snuggled closer still. Why? She didn't know.
It wasn't a nice sound. The growl was guttural and
rough, so nasty most people would've deployed self-
preservation like a parachute. But as the sound came
again, a steady rumbling purr, it registered as reas-

suring instead of frightening, helpful instead of harm-
ful, soothing and—

The earth swayed.

Her body followed, interrupting her train of
thought. Or rather, her trip down the rabbit hole. A
good explanation. Clearly, she'd lost her mind.
Nothing else explained the brain drift or her sudden
contentment. The emotional shift made no sense—
must be a fallacy. A story spun in an endorphin-fueled
cloud of euphoria to distract her from the fact she
couldn't feel her legs anymore.

As physical awareness faded, Elise accepted reality.
She wasn't tethered to her body anymore. Pain severed
the connection, giving her a clear message—she was
going to die. Impending doom loomed like a crow, its
repetitive caw sounding like a death knell as her muscles numbed and her mind faded.

"Lass." The deep voice rolled through her. A jar-
ring bump. The sound of flapping. A fresh burst of
pain. The cold rush of air as something rustled. "Look
at me."

The command pierced through the mind fog. As it
swirled, leaving clear patches in its wake, Elise tried to
obey. He spoke again. She clung to his voice, using it
as a lifeline, trying to raise her lashes. Her body refused to cooperate. Her eyes remained shut.

"Shite," the voice said, coming from far away.
"Hang on, *talmina*."

"Who?"

"Cyprus."

"I know you."

"Aye, you do." Gentle hands touched her. "Open
your eyes for me."

Elise tried again, but as he picked her up, the fog

became too thick. She couldn't fight her way through it. "Can't."

"Then give me your name."

She whispered it to him.

"Elise—stay awake. Stay with me."

She wanted to listen. Needed to stay connected to the sound of his voice, but as the world shifted, she lost her bearings, falling head long into darkness. Into an abyss that reached up and swallowed her whole.

9

C rouched in the driveway with Elise in his
arms, Cyprus scanned the front of the house.
Ancient stone façade. Tall rectangular windows with the curtains drawn. No lights on inside. No
vehicles in the circular drive rimmed by massive trees.
Cyprus growled in approval. A summer home abandoned for the winter by its human owners.

The perfect place to take Elise.

The smell of wet leaves in the air, he pushed to his
feet with her cradled against him and searched his
surroundings one more time. No danger lurking in the
shadows behind the row of shrubs. No rogues in pursuit in the storm darkened sky behind him. He released a pent-up breath. Safe enough for now. Maybe
for the rest of the night. Maybe just for an hour. Either
way, would work. He required time, enough to assess
the extent of Elise's injuries and determine his next
step.

Dragon half still hunting for unseen threats, he
headed for the front entrance. Flanked by huge urns,
the portico acted like a beacon, ornate pillars
gleaming beneath the faint fall of moonlight, guiding
him toward the main walkway. Gravel crunching be-

neath his boots, he glanced around again, then down at Elise. So pretty. So pale. Drifting in and out of consciousness. Her breathing far too shallow.

Steadying her with one arm, he cupped her chin. His thumb settled against her pulse point and...shite. Not strong enough. Despite his best efforts—his attempts to stabilize her in flight—her heart continued to slow, the beat becoming more sluggish by the moment.

One eye on the front door, the rest of his attention on her, he kept his feet moving and called on magic. Heat crested like a wave, the dark flow feverish as he linked to her bio-energy. Her aura flared bright for second, then settled into a gentle glow. Fear tightened his chest. Goddess help him. Elise was in serious trouble. Her vital signs plummeting so fast he didn't know if he could pull her back from the brink before she bottomed out. Before she depleted the last of her energy reserves. Before the long, slow slide toward death became irreversible.

Cyprus sprinted across the driveway.

Elise whimpered. He murmured, hoping to soothe her, but didn't slow down. As much as he hated hurting her, she could handle a little more pain. What she couldn't afford was anymore delays. He needed her out of her clothes and tucked up against him—full body contact, skin on skin. The simple touch of his hands would no longer be enough.

Reaching the flagstone path, he raced toward the front steps. He glanced down and...his heart fisted inside his chest. She looked worse, the pallor of her skin so white it appeared translucent. Desperation made him move even faster. Knees pumping, he took the stairs three at a time. Elise cried out, twisting in his arms. He kept going and, crossing the portico, unleashed a torrent of magic. Multiple deadbolts groaned a second before the door blew open. The heavy wood panel hit the interior wall with a bang and swung back toward him.

Quick feet helped him avoid the backlash.

A quicker survey of the entry hall turned him left beneath a wide archway. His gaze swept the space. High, tall windows hidden behind silk curtains. A stone fireplace living large in the center of the longest wall. A square-backed couch, a cluster of armchairs, coffee and side tables, the entire lot draped by white sheets. Cyprus nodded. Living room, no question...a good place to strip Elise and assess her injuries.

Oriental rug underfoot, he sidestepped an ottoman. Not bothering to remove the sheet, he laid her down on the couch. Plush seat cushions softened beneath her.

Her eyelashes flickered. He caught a flash of blue before she closed her eyes again. "Cyprus."

"Aye, lass. Hang on. Hang on for me," he said, his fear for her so sharp pain streaked through him. "Almost there."

"I want to go home," she whispered, her words broken.

"I know, *talmina*."

"Now? Can I go now?"

Cyprus wanted to say "no". The need to tell her the truth—that he would never let her go, that she would never again be far from his side—knocked through him. He quelled the urge. Honesty would have its day, but the time wasn't now and the place wasn't here. "Not yet."

She whimpered.

He gripped both lapels and, with a vicious yank, ripped her coat open. Fat buttons flew in all directions, bouncing off the closest table, flying over the couch back, hitting the wooden floor with high-pitched pings. He didn't care. The house could fall down around him and he still wouldn't stop. He needed his hands on her. Now and...goddamn it, he should have flown faster. Found a safe place to land quicker. Something. Anything. It should have been five minutes ago, but with the storm raging, he'd done the best with what he'd been given.

On one knee beside the couch, he wrestled her out of her coat, pulled the boots off her feet, and tugged her jeans down her legs. Her sweater came off next. Her underwear followed and—

"Fucking hell." So much blood. Cuts and bruises all over her. And her leg...Jesus. With magic feeding him information, he knew it was broken, her femur cracked in two places.

With clenched teeth and gentle hands, Cyprus turned her onto her side. Shock made him flinch. He sucked in a quick breath. Dear goddess, her back...her lower back...Grizgunn had sliced her wide open. He stared at the gaping hole for a moment. His dragon half snarled at him, telling him to hurry, shoving his mounting fury out of the way. *Save it for later. Later*, for when he got his claws on the bastard. Right now, only one thing mattered—Elise. His female needed him to stay on task.

His hand pressed to the wound, he murmured a spell. Heat gathered in his palm as his clothes disappeared. Fuck modesty. To hell with civility. He didn't have time for polite and proper. Naked was better. Full body contact worked best when feeding a female. But first, he needed Elise to link in and accept what he offered.

Lifting her into his arms, Cyprus took her place on

the couch. He settled in her his lap, then swung his feet up and laid back, stretching out with her on top of him. Soft breasts met his chest. Her belly resting against his, he spread his legs, allowing space for both of hers between his. The movement jarred her. She mewled in protest. Whispering an apology, he kept one hand against the wound on her back and cupped her nape with the other.

She twitched, fighting his control.

He held firm and, pressing her cheek to his chest, called on the Meridian. A whirlwind started inside his head. He banged on the gateway again, requesting access to the source of all living things. Please, Goddess...let it work. He'd never fed a female before. When near a female he always took, opening the connection to take what he needed—the nourishment that kept him healthy and strong. What he attempted now was new to him. Instead of taking energy, he wanted to give it, to heal instead of feed and—

The door inside his mind slammed open. The rush hit him like a drug, the impact so intoxicating his mind blurred. Everything went fuzzy. His eyes closed. Pleasure streamed through him, wiping his mental slate clean and...huh. What the hell had just happened? Fighting through the mind fog, Cyprus frowned. He should be doing something, shouldn't he? The question struck like a spiked hammer. He waffled a moment, trying to get his bearings.

Soft skin shifted against his.

Mental acuity surged back to the forefront.

Bloody hell. Elise.

Stabilizing the flow, Cyprus grabbed it by the tail. He looped it end over end, controlling the current, increasing its potency, all his focus on Elise. Power snaked through his veins, enclosing him in magical splendor. He held it in a firm grip, allowed the pressure to build, then let it go, channeling every ounce of energy in Elise's direction.

She jerked against him. Her spine arched. He kept her in place, willing her to accept the connection. She made a small sound of distress, fighting the infusion.

"Please, *talmina*," he whispered against the top of her head.

Reaching out with his mind, he attempted to touch hers. She'd heard him before. Had listened to him in the cathedral. Maybe she would this time too. Cyprus needed her to accept him. He couldn't force the life bond. Energy-fuse required a female's cooperation. If Elise refused him, she would die without ever waking up. Without ever truly meeting him.

Holding her tighter, he mind-spoke, pushing the plea from his head into hers. *"Elise, donnae fight it. Take from me."*

His voice stilled her mid-struggle. Forehead now pressed to the middle of his chest, she stayed in place as he spoke to her again. The whisper simmered in the air between them. A crease formed between her brows. He gentled his touch, caressing her nape, her shoulder, the length of her arm. With each stroke of his hand, she relaxed a little more. Raising his head, Cyprus nudged her with his chin. She turned toward him. He set his mouth against her temple. The energy stream amplified, and she took a deep breath, softening against him.

"There we go. Come on, baby...open up, let me in," he said, staying with mind-speak, praying she not only responded, but obeyed.

A heartbeat passed.

Worry trickled in.

He asked again. Another second and—

He sensed the shift. The bond formed, holding him captive as Elise took control of the connection. Healing energy surged from him into her. Heat exploded through him. Bliss followed, making him groan as she drank deep and hummed in pleasure. Her aura started to glow hot and bright, warming her skin, knitting sinew and bone, repairing her kidney and relieving the worst of her pain. It would be hours yet before she was fully healed, but God, what a way to spend it—skin to skin and heart to heart with the female meant to be his.

Murmuring to her, Cyprus pressed soft kisses to her temple. Thank God. He'd done it. Fused with a female and claimed his mate. Elise may not know it yet, but she now belonged to him. She would feel the bond they now shared the second she woke in his arms. Energy-fuse was a powerful force: tying hearts, minds and lives together, forming a bond that lasted a lifetime and could never be broken.

Contentment washed through him.

With a sigh, Cyprus grabbed the sheet draped over the back of the couch. He tugged, flipping the cotton forward, covering Elise from shoulders to toes. She didn't need it for warmth. As a fire dragon, his core temperature always ran hot. The heat he gave off would sustain them both, but...

Duty called.

As much as he wanted to wallow in the feel of his female, it was time. He must let his warriors know where he'd landed. Wallaig would get nasty if he didn't, so...time to reassert his command.

Rechecking the energy flow, he urged Elise to take more. She obeyed, her greed a steady draw that made him hum in approval. Good. She was all right. Not quite out of danger, but on automatic pilot, drinking deep, assuaging her thirst, taking all he fed her.

Careful not to disturb her, he opened mind-speak. *"Wallaig."*

"Do you have her?"

"Aye. She's badly injured, but—"

"Energy-fuse?"

"Up and running. She's feeding now."

Wallaig chuckled. *"Lucky bastard."*

Cyprus smiled. No question. Why the goddess had gifted him with someone so precious, he didn't know. No way to understand it. He wasn't even going to try. *"The rogues?"*

"In retreat," Wallaig said. *"Kruger and Levin are giving chase."*

"Nay, Wallaig, pull them back." The sound of wings flapping interrupted the connection. Static hissed, swirling over his temples before Wallaig came back on line. *"Rein Levin and Kruger in and meet me here. I donnae think Elise will be ready tae fly before dawn, which means we spend the day."*

"Pretty name for a female. Is she as pretty in person?"

"Prettier."

His friend snorted. *"Location?"*

"Fifty miles north of the firth. A human's summer home."

A pause. A ping echoed inside his head as Wallaig tracked him. *"Got you. Be there in a bit."*

"Good."

He wanted the extra protection. A lethal guard in the house and checking the perimeter. With the rogues in full retreat, he probably wouldn't need it, but a warrior could never be too careful. Grizgunn might be an arsehole, but he didn't seem stupid.

The realization should have pleased him. A cunning enemy, after all, made for a more challenging opponent. Was a lot more fun too. But with Elise in the mix, he refused to take chances. She came first now. Her wellbeing trumped chasing down his enemies. Grizgunn had gotten lucky. The rogue pack had just been given a pass.

At least, for tonight.

The second he secured Elise inside his mountain lair, he would show no mercy...and the bastards would pay.

10

Low murmurs came from far away, through a long tunnel filled with murky shadows. The darkness felt thick, as though it had substance and she'd been swaddled in feather-down. Or buried under a mountain of cotton balls.

The idea should've disturbed her. Elise found it oddly comforting instead. The even drumbeat helped, echoing in her ear, vibrating inside her head, helping her surface a little at a time. A slow, steady crawl. A meandering incline, one she ascended, yet didn't feel quite real.

Something to be concerned about or embrace?

Adrift on a sea of feel-good, Elise couldn't decide. It seemed too far away to worry about—a mild worry at most, a pesky irritant at worst. Her chest rose and fell. In. Out. Easy inhales. Relaxed exhales, perfection as she crested through thick, fluffy layers only to be pulled back under as something cupped her shoulder. Each gentle pass came with a current. Heat washed in, lapping at her, sinking into her muscles, drawing out the aches and pains, smoothing her worries like a hot iron over wrinkled fabric.

Steamrolled. Pressed flat. Without a care in the world.

Such a nice change, considering her night and what had happened.

The thought prickled through her. She came up another level as the fine hairs on her nape rose in warning. Like the encroaching tide, awareness crept in, eroding contentment, piercing through her peace. Elise frowned, trying to get her bearings. Crap. Nothing but blur. Her eyes refused to focus, but as her mind sharpened, a feeling of impending doom poked at her. *What had happened...what had happened...what the hell had happened?* A good question. The perfect one to ask given something frightening lingered in the fringes of her mind. A shadow memory, one so hazy she could tell it was there, but when she reached out, couldn't touch it.

Elise tried again.

The rough edges unraveled. She tugged on the mental strings.

A name surfaced. *Cyprus.*

"Here, talmina."

The whispered words unfurled. She jolted upright.

"Shh, now," he murmured, sounding close. "Easy, lass."

"What?" Her hands flew out to the side and landed on something hard. Something warm. Something that moved up and down, in and out. "Where?"

A large hand cupped her face. "I've got you, Elise. You're all right."

Scottish accent. Calloused hands. The strong pull of swirling current beneath her skin, the heat as seductive as the timbre of his voice. Recognition slammed through her. Her eyes flew open and...Christ on a cracker. She still couldn't see a thing. Blinking rapid-fire, she fought to clear her vision. He murmured to her again. She jerked her head back. Her focus narrowed, then came back on line. Tanned skin. Broad shoulders. A muscular chest. Comprehension struck. Cyprus, in all his high-octane glory.

She stared a moment before her gaze rose, skimming over a corded neck, a strong jaw, and a too-gorgeous-for-words mouth before colliding with a pale, purple gaze.

Elise sucked in a startled breath, realizing two things at once. One (and perhaps the most daunting), she sat in Cyprus's lap, arms the size of tree trunks around her. And two (and no less urgent), she needed to move her ass, get up and go before—

"Donnae move."

His gaze trapped hers, sparking in warning, and she froze. *Dragon*. She was sitting on a dragon. Or rather, a guy who turned into a dragon. Not that she understood how it worked, but really what more did she need to know besides *dragon*.

"You...you're a..." She trailed off, unable to voice the word. Somehow, that would make it real, which was...moronic. Elise wanted to kick herself. Denying what she'd seen—and experienced—wouldn't help. "I saw you."

"Lucky for you."

She blinked, not understanding. "Lucky?"

"Aye. Not many humans are fortunate enough to witness Dragonkind in full flight."

Elise opened her mouth, then closed it again. *Dragonkind?* Really? That was a thing? A real species present in the world? The idea seemed insane. Although, the 'in full flight' aspect had certainly been spectacular. Better than any book she'd ever read.

Which was...well, she didn't know exactly. She wanted to say awesome. Fascinating would work too, but...

"You were on fire," she whispered, staring at him in astonishment.

His lips twitched. Placing a finger beneath her chin, he closed her mouth. "That happens sometimes. When I get angry."

"You're not angry now, are you?"

"Nay." His fingertips stroked along her jaw, making her shiver, making her want more of his warmth. "You're safe from my fire, Elise. No matter what form I take, I will never harm you."

"Oh," she said, not sure how to react. *Safe with him.* The thought went nine rounds inside her head. All right, yes...strange as it seemed, she believed him. Her faith didn't stem from anything proven. The conviction he told the truth was abstract, more of a feeling, as though the deepest, darkest part of her knew—just *knew*—her trust in him would never be misplaced. "You're one of the good guys?"

"With you—always. With my enemies—never."

Simple words. Lethal meaning. A little bit scary, a whole lot hot.

Elise swallowed, finding him as fascinating as she did dangerous. Which wasn't the least bit advisable. Fascination should be the last thing on her mind. Escape should be the first, and yet Elise didn't want to run. Despite what she knew—that he was vicious and different—Cyprus drew her like bees to flowers. Not normal at all, and as his thumb brushed over her bottom lip and goose bumps pebbled her skin, she abandoned prudent in favor of curiosity. Now, all she wanted to do was learn more.

"You have questions, lass. Ask."

The perfect opening, but as she held his gaze, her thoughts refused to form.

Patient in the face of her silence, he leaned back against the couch, giving her more space to think. It didn't work. The movement shifted her in his lap, making her aware of her body against his and—

Her butt brushed across his thighs.

Shock shivered through her. Dear lord, how had she missed the fact she sat butt naked in his lap: as in bare as the day she'd been born *naked*. All right, so he'd covered her with a sheet, but...

Heat flushed through her, and not the appropriate kind either. Had she been thinking straight, she would've labeled her reaction *indecent*. Except that wasn't the word she wanted to use. Decadent. Delectable. Downright delicious. Yes, *that*...those words seemed much more in line with the obscene suggestions turning her brain into a racetrack.

Her libido yee-hawed and revved its engine, roaring onto the circuit before Elise could protest. She tried to slam on the brakes, but gosh darn it all, her race car named Desire was gone. Already at high speed imagining all the interesting ways Cyprus could drive her to the edge of passion, and beyond.

"What the...you can't just...holy crap," she muttered, trying not to squirm in his lap. She needed to protest...right now...before she did something stupid, like lick him. Planting her hands on his chest, she shoved, retreating even as she marveled at his strength. "Let me up."

His grip on her firmed. "Nay, I like you where you are."

At a loss for words, Elise huffed.

His eyes crinkled at the corners.

Hers narrowed on him. "Listen, Cyprus. I'm not—"

"Oh, but you are," he murmured, keeping her in place against him. "You like being in my arms, *talmina*."

The endearment gave her an absurd amount of pleasure.

She scowled at him. Enough of that. The arrogant jerk. How dare he tell her how she felt. Cyprus didn't have a clue, except—he wasn't lying. Or even a little off base. She liked the feel of him. Was enjoying being so close and...God. He was gorgeous. Magnificent in dark and dangerous ways. A man's man—masculine, hard-bodied, the kind of guy who made a woman's heart pound just by looking at him. And the kind who rarely, if ever, looked her way. Not that she didn't deserve his attention. She was pretty enough. Liked herself just fine, but most men preferred sexy and curvy and flirty.

Sad to say, but the universe hadn't waved its magic wand over her. Nope. Not even close. She'd gotten the short end of that stick. Didn't embody natural grace or put-together perfection, never mind have the ability to turn on a hip-swinging, pouty-lipped act. She'd gotten the book worm gene instead, preferring libraries to bars and solitude to other people's company. A fact Amantha lamented every time her friend wanted her to dress up and go out.

The thought closed her throat, then her mouth. As the silence stretched, she couldn't think of a single, intelligent thing to say. So typical. Completely unfair. She always choked in front of hot guys.

"A wee bit stymied, are you?"

"Or maybe it's a standoff." Elise blinked, surprised the snarky comment had come out of her mouth. *Thank you, brain.* Finally. A comeback to put in the non-stupid column.

He raised a brow. "You staring me down?"

"Could be."

"Think you'll win?"

While naked beneath a sheet he controlled? Elise swallowed a snort. Fat chance. Intuition told her she wouldn't be winning *anything* until she put her clothes back on. "No, but I can't just let you walk all over me. That must be a Dragonkind law, or something."

He laughed. "You're going tae be trouble, I can tell."

The approval in his eyes stroked over her. Her heart hitched. Wow, a compliment. A sincere one. How Elise knew, she wasn't sure, but somehow, she sensed his admiration. The truth was right there, shimmering in the air between them, so close she perceived it first and saw it second. And as she drank his appreciation in like a plant too long without water, awe circled, making her chest go tight.

He brushed the hair away from her face. "All right, lass?"

She swallowed past the lump in her throat. "I don't know. I feel strange."

"Completely normal," he said, watching her. "It'll take you some time tae adjust."

"To what?"

"Me. Energy-fuse. Plus, you've more healing yet tae do."

Healing? Elise frowned. She'd been hurt? The question sparked a hidden memory. She sucked in a quick breath. The cathedral. The attack. That god awful blue dragon. Her hand flew to her shoulder. Smooth skin, no longer torn open by sharp teeth and the brutal slice of claws. Remembered pain jolted through her. Twisting away from Cyprus, she checked her back. Same story: no cuts, no blood, nothing but healed skin a little sensitive to the touch.

"God." Elise tried to scramble off his lap. She needed to check—

"Be still, lass," he said, preventing her flight from his arms.

"Let go." Panic made her push against him. "I have to go. I have to—"

"Let me hold you."

She shook her head.

His arm tightened around her shoulders. The large hand wrapped over the top of her thigh flexed. "Donnae press me, lass. I'll not let you go yet. Your leg isn't healed."

"Not healed?" she asked with a squeak, sounding like a mouse being eaten by a cat. "It's broken?"

"In two places."

"Grizgunn."

"Aye." Purple irises shimmering, Cyprus bared his teeth on a growl. "The bloody bastard. I'm going tae rip his guts out his spine when I find him."

A shiver of fear rumbled through her. "You're going after him?"

"He hurt you. He dies."

The violent promise in his eyes should've scared her. It didn't. His fierceness reassured her instead. Something in his tone, something on his face, the determined set of his jaw confirmed what she already knew—she was safe with him. Despite her misgivings and all the dragon craziness, Cyprus spoke the truth. He would never hurt her. But even better? He would defend her too.

Disbelief welled deep inside her.

No one had ever fought for her before. Not even her parents. Tough love ruled in her house: *solve your own problems.* How many times had she heard that growing up? Been left alone when she'd needed someone to help? Always. Over and over. No one had been there to take the brunt, never mind sought to right a wrong on her behalf.

But Cyprus would. In a heartbeat. Without really knowing her.

The unexpected gift gripped her heart and squeezed. Gratitude and astonishment leaked out, filling her so full tears stung her eyes.

The vicious glint in Cyprus's gaze softened. Drawing her closer, he tucked her head beneath his chin. "Go ahead, *talmina*—cry. You've earned the right. I'll wait."

Elise tried to huff in annoyance. The sound got stuck inside her chest. Absurd. She didn't need his permission to cry. But as she fisted her hands in the sheet, struggling to stay strong, determined to keep it together, she realized—maybe she did need permission to let go. To let it ride and allow the hurt to escape, instead of shoving it back down like she always did.

The first sob surprised her.

The second broke through the barrier, forcing her to turn into his embrace instead of away. Cyprus murmured in approval, and as her first tear fell, praised her courage, telling her she was wonderful, that he was proud of her, holding her so tight he made her breakdown seem understandable. Normal, even.

His acceptance was the last straw. And as the flood gates opened, Elise cried even as she wondered what the hell he'd done to her...and what on earth he would do next.

11

All cried out, Elise rested in his arms, her bottom in his lap, her cheek pressed to his chest. Each of her hitching breaths pinched at his heart. Poor lass. She'd sobbed herself into exhaustion. Cyprus didn't blame her. After the night she'd had, she deserved some crying time. Some screaming time too if she needed it. Most females would after an impromptu skydive without a parachute. Learning dragons lived inside their tidy little world sucked for humans. Being attacked by one was even worse.

Not that she appreciated the basic truth of it.

Such a stubborn lass. So courageous, he couldn't help but admire her. She'd tried so hard to tuck all that emotion away: to hide her hurt, deny her shock and banish her fear. A strong female. A gorgeous one who disliked weakness, wanting to stay strong, not break down, but...fuck. He was glad she had—beyond proud she trusted him enough to give him those tears. Her vulnerability touched a part of him he hadn't known existed, filling him so full, contentment spilled over his rough edges.

Smoothed out. Well rested and relaxed for the first time in ages.

Every bit of it Elise's doing.

Cyprus sighed and, sliding into a comfortable slouch on the couch, cuddled her closer. Tipping his head back, he stretched his legs out and closed his eyes. The personality of the century-old house enveloped him. The soft creak of solid walls. The patter of rain against antique window panes behind thick curtains. The quiet toll of the grandfather clock standing guard in the entry hall. He counted each chime, wondering about the time.

Mid-afternoon, most likely. Elise had slept a long time. So had he, the hypnotic draw of feeding her soothing him as he slumbered.

He could still feel it, the gentle syphoning as Elise took, and he gave. She needed more yet. Her leg required attention. Although, he'd plucked out the splinters, fitting bone chips together like puzzle pieces, her femur needed time to knit. Turning inward, he called on his magic, assessing the damage and what had already been repaired. Lit up on his mental screen, the fractures appeared like dark cracks on white bone. He frowned. Not quite healed, but that would change. With his life force connected to hers, his dragon half supervised the energy infusion, coaxing Elise to take more, ensuring she got what she needed. So, it wouldn't be long. An hour, three at most, and his female's leg would be good as new.

The clock tolled four bells.

Cyprus forced his eyes open. Four PM. Time to move. He wanted to get out of the living room, and Elise into the shower, before his warriors woke for the day. Not that he didn't trust his brothers-in-arms. The males under his command were solid, as honorable as he was protective. None would ever hurt a female—or touch one that didn't belong to them—but that didn't mean the wankers wouldn't look...and appreciate.

The thought left a bad taste in his mouth.

Elise belonged to him. Which meant he must get her moving. No way would he introduce her to his warriors while wrapped in naught more than a sheer excuse for a sheet.

Gathering the thin cotton in one hand, he wrapped it over her legs and nudged her with his chin. Tendrils of her hair brushed against his skin. The scent of vanilla and crushed almonds rose. Hmm, yum —she smelled delicious, like fresh baked cookies and the creamer he put in his coffee every day. Humming in pleasure, he did it again, rubbing the strands along his jaw, over his mouth and—

She grumbled at him. His mouth curved. So pretty. Beyond precious. A sleepy female not ready to get up for the day.

He would've liked to appease her. Cuddling her all evening seemed like an excellent idea. Shite, holding her was no hardship, but as Cyprus heard a thump above his head, he knew Levin's feet had just hit the floor. Somewhere up on the third floor of the house, Kruger was no doubt doing the same. And Wallaig? He fine-tuned his sonar, picking up trace energy, tracking the unique signal his first in command dropped like napalm in his wake and...ah, right there. Camped out in the kitchen, no doubt laid out on the floor guarding the rear entrance.

"Elise?"

"Hmm?" She tipped her head back. Out of focus, bloodshot eyes met his. She blinked, wet lashes forming perfect triangles against her skin.

"Fair warning, lass. We're moving."

She frowned.

Cyprus didn't wait for the objection he saw spark in her eyes to develop. Only an idiot waited to be scolded, so instead of asking, he gathered her up and pushed to his feet. Cradled in his arms, she squeaked in alarm. He almost smiled, but stopped at that last second. Laughing at her wouldn't win him any points, and an angry female would be harder to deal with, never mind hold. And goddess, he wanted to continue holding her. She felt like heaven against him: soft and curvy, warm and pleasing, sheer perfection as he skirted the end of the couch and headed for the large archway. "Hold on tae me, *talmina*."

"Put me down, Cyprus. I can walk."

"Not yet. You can try in an hour or two. Until then, you keep your weight on your good leg." Treating her to a no-nonsense look, he jostled her a wee bit. "Agreed?"

Chewing on her bottom lip, no doubt trying to decide whether to listen, she wiggled her toes and bent her knee. Her mouth tightened, broadcasting her pain. His gut clenched, then relaxed again when she slid her arm around his neck. "Guess I'm not all better yet, eh?"

"It takes time."

"Not a whole lot. I mean, it's amazing I feel as well as I do, considering..." The strain in her voice strung him tight. Inhaling deep, she exhaled slow and, smoothing the sheet, rubbed the top of her injured thigh. Once...twice...a third stroke before she abandoned the soothing motion and looked up at him. "How did you do it?"

"What—heal you?" Looking both ways, he stepped into the main hallway.

"Yeah." A shadow entered her eyes, dimming the

blue. "There was a lot of blood. I remember thinking my kidney was probably gone. I think..." She paused. He watched her throat work and felt his own tighten. "I'm pretty sure I should be dead."

"I would never have allowed that tae happen," he said, his chest hurting at the thought. "You were mine the moment I spoke tae you inside the church, Elise."

"Another mystery." She shook her head, no doubt trying to puzzle out mind-speak...and the connection she now shared with him. "I have so many questions."

"Good. I will answer them all, but first..." Footfalls softened by a runner, he walked down a narrow corridor. Five doors. Cyprus nudged each one open with naught more than a thought, looking for the bathroom on the main level of the house. He knew it was here. Old houses followed predictable patterns, the floor plans easy to guess and...the last door on the right yielded results. Shoving the wood panel with his bare foot, he crossed the threshold. Big room with a large shower. Black and white tiles. Fully renovated. Perfect for his purposes. "Let's get you cleaned up."

"God, yes. I could use a shower." The eagerness in her voice cleared the heaviness from his heart. She pointed to the bathmat in front of the glass door. "If you put me down over there and turn on the water, I'll just—"

He chuckled. A nice try, but no chance she would be getting her way. Or he would be leaving her to bathe alone. "I'll not be putting you down, lass."

Her grip on his neck tightened. "What?"

No need to answer. Elise would learn what he planned soon enough.

Releasing her legs, he allowed her feet to touch the floor. She wobbled. He steadied her, making sure she balanced on her good leg before tugging on the sheet.

The cotton slipped off her shoulders, exposing the graceful curve of her back.

She made a frantic grab for the covering. "Hey!"

He pulled again.

A death grip on the sheet, she shook her head.

"I've seen every inch of you already, Elise. I stroked you while you slept, enjoyed the softness of your skin, the fine curve of your hips and the taste of your energy. Jesus, lass. You're gorgeous."

Hot color stole into her cheeks. She opened her mouth, closed it again.

His lips curved. He knew he shouldn't be enjoying her embarrassment, but well...hey. Might as well admit it. He liked her modesty along with the slow rise of her blush. "Let go, Elise. Let me look at you. Allow me the pleasure of bathing with you."

Color still high, blue eyes as big as saucers, she stared at him. He tugged the sheet again. Her grip loosened. A second later, she allowed it to fall, and he hummed in approval. Bloody hell. He wanted to lick her all over, staring with the trim, blond curls between her thighs.

His dragon growled, liking the plan.

Cyprus shut it down. Elise needed gentle reassurance, not an intense brute plagued by lusty thoughts. At least, not right now. Today wasn't the time for laying her down and loving her hard. Mayhap later, after he'd taken her a few times—after he owned all her trust—she might enjoy a bit of rough bed play, but not tonight.

Trailing his fingertips over her collar bone, he cupped her shoulder, turned her around and...goddess help him. Her arse was as gorgeous as the rest of her, round and pert, just the right size for his hands. Pushing the length of her hair over one shoulder, he stoked along her spine. His hand slid over her lower back, testing the skin, checking her kidney, looking for any problems. A wee bit red yet, but the spot she'd been sliced open looked good. One hundred percent healed.

Brushing over her hip, he flattened his palm against her belly. She sucked in a startled breath. He whispered in her ear. "Such a good lass, letting me touch as I like."

"Cyprus—"

"You're beautiful, Elise. Like a fairy princess come tae life, so sweet and curvy. Perfect beneath my hands."

The rigidity of her spine softened. "I'm not perfect."

He cupped her cheek. Caressing her softly, he brushed over her bottom lip. "You are tae me."

Tears filled her eyes.

Dipping his head, he kissed her gently. Such a sensitive lass, not at all accustomed to compliments. He would change that—tell her every damn day she was beautiful if only to see the wonder he saw blooming on her face right now. Unable to resist, he nipped her lip. Elise gasped. He soothed the wee sting with his tongue, licking at her mouth as he unleashed magic and cranked the tap facets. The pipes jerked before the water came on, falling from the shower head in a steady stream. Cyprus tested it with his mind. Too cold. He adjusted the temperature, warming each droplet, ensuring Elise's comfort before opening the door.

One arm curled around her, he nudged her forward. "In you go, lass."

"I can wash myself," she said, voice soft, without an ounce of conviction.

"Why bother when you've got me tae do it?"

Kissing her one more time, he lifted her over the threshold and stepped in behind her. Warm water hit her in a fine spray and splashed onto him. Reveling in the slippery slide of her, he tipped her head back and wet her hair. She relaxed, leaning against him, allowing him to help her balance on one foot.

He murmured his appreciation. The beginnings of trust. A good start, one that would carry him through the rest of evening and into hard truths in need of telling.

A conversation was in order. He must reveal all and tell her about his kind. About energy-fuse, and the fact he'd mated her without asking for permission first. About Grizgunn too. The bastard had more than just hurt her. He'd ingested her energy, absorbing the unique signal Elise wore like a second skin. Now, she couldn't return home and hope to stay safe.

His enemies would track her the second she left his protection. As a high-energy female, his mate would be coveted by Dragonkind males the world over, and Grizgunn wasn't stupid. He wouldn't pass up a second attempt to take her. Which meant Elise's safety now relied on her proximity to him.

Unfair? No question. But real life didn't play by the rules.

He could only shield her so far. The life she knew was over. Goodbye human world, hello Dragonkind. The thought gave him pause. Worry poked at him. Cyprus pursed his lips and picked up the soap, wondering how best to tell Elise about her change in status, 'cause sure as shite, the second he revealed the truth, he knew his female would balk. And he'd be in for the fight of his life to keep her with him.

12

D ressed in comfortable sweats, Elise sat alone at the dining room table, one thought circling like vultures over a dead body. She couldn't go home...ever.

Not if she wanted to stay alive.

Amantha was going to kill her.

Pain and regret tumbled through her as she thought of her best friend. She'd been there through thick and thin, a constant source of laughter and support. God, she was going to miss her snarky attitude. Her warped sense of humor and big-hearted generosity too. Throat gone tight, Elise set her elbow on the table and her chin in her palm. Maybe she could find a way to contact Amantha. Let her know that she was all right, not lying dead in a ditch somewhere. Her friend deserved to know. She didn't want her to worry, and Amantha would boil over without news. Pace herself silly, eat too many sweets waiting for Elise to get in touch.

Maybe she should mention it to Cyprus. A phone call wouldn't hurt, would it?

Elise chewed on the question, wondering what he

would say...and if she'd be safe doing anything in the human world.

Cyprus didn't pull any punches. Or make any bones about how dangerous Edinburgh would be for her now. He'd been honest to the point of bluntness, explaining about Grizgunn and the asshole's ability to track her if she left the safety Cyprus and his pack provided.

Talk about a fist to the solar plexus. An hour had passed since the big reveal: talk of energy feedings and magical talents, the ability to shift between human and dragon form...her importance as a high-energy female in the Dragonkind world.

The concept shook her foundation, yet made her feel special too. Worthy. Deserving of attention. Important to someone. Truly *seen* for the first time in years. It was as though she'd been waiting her entire life for someone to lift the veil and hand her the information.

Which was weird. Not at all the right reaction.

She should be running, screaming, freaking out in major ways. All she'd managed so far was an upset stomach. Elise frowned at the paisley table cloth. Ugly swirling pattern. Gaudy color combination. Zero panic in sight. Just a terrible case of indigestion as reality sank in, then reached out to nudge her. Again. For what seemed like the millionth time since Cyprus lifted her out of the shower, dried her off, and dressed her with nothing but a thought.

Swallowing the awful taste in her mouth, Elise smoothed her hand over the sleeve of her dark orange sweatshirt. It was insane. Barely believable at all. He'd conjured clothes for her out of thin air. With nothing more than the wave of his hand.

Magic, he said.

A whole lot of crazy town, she thought (very quietly) to herself.

No sense voicing her opinion and insulting him. After all Cyprus had done for her—holding her throughout the day, healing her injuries, letting her cry all over him—upsetting him somehow seemed rude. Like the worse sort of affront. Elise huffed. Not the Canadian way at all. Her countrymen would be appalled and—

Her imbecilic train of thought proved it. She'd clearly lost her mind. Or what little remained of it, worrying more about hurting Cyprus's feelings than finding a way home.

"*Talmina*."

Jumping in her chair, her head snapped toward the door.

Two plates in hand, Cyprus stood beneath the archway, so tall the top of his head brushed the lintel, so broad his shoulders blocked her view into the kitchen. Pale purple eyes met hers. "You're stewing again."

"Can you blame me?" she asked, her gaze drifting over him. A frisson of excitement shivered through her. Man, get a load of him. He did something serious for her. She loved looking at him. Wanted to be back in the shower with her hands on him again. A sinking sensation pooled in her belly, vibrating between her hipbones. Pressing her thighs together, Elise cleared her throat, fighting to keep herself on task and her mind out of the gutter. "I just learned I'm food for Dragonkind."

"Not Dragonkind, just me." His mouth curved as he walked toward her. Desire in his eyes, he looked her over, making her want and crave without laying a hand on her. "And what a pretty feast you make."

"Okay, that's not helpful." She squirmed in her seat. "I'm supposed to be thinking here, figuring things out, not—"

"Lusting? Imagining the hot slide of my tongue over your skin?"

"That's...you...good grief." Heat rocketed through her, blooming in unwise places. She scowled at him. "Do you have an off button?"

"Nay. Not when it comes tae you." Grinning like an evil sex god, he set a plate down in front of her. Placing the other dish to her left, he planted his hand on the tabletop and leaned over her.

Unable to stop herself, Elise tipped her chin up. Her lips parted.

With a growl, he accepted the invitation and, fisting his fingers in her hair, invaded her mouth. He took it deep, stroking her with his tongue, delivering his taste, giving her a contact high along with the pleasure. Her heart throbbed. Blood rushed in her ears, making her lightheaded. When she moaned, he drew away, gentling his grip, treating her to soft kisses instead of deep possession.

Breathing hard, his mouth a hair's breadth from hers, he hummed. "Fuck, you're delicious. You make me forget myself."

"More," she whispered, addicted to his taste. "Kiss me again."

Cyprus shook his head and, releasing her hair, retreated. "Eat, lass. We'll get to the sex soon enough."

Sex. Sex with Cyprus.

The thought shivered through her. Libidinous greed followed, running circles around her. Going to bed with him wouldn't be polite. It would be down and dirty, hot and sweaty, so intense he would no doubt blow her mind. But wow, what a way to go. Elise nearly groaned as her imagination spun in dangerous directions. Round and round, one lust-fueled revolution churned into another, making desire rise so hard she couldn't sit still, forcing her to admit...

She wanted him...badly. So much she ached in tender places.

Taking a seat, Cyprus tapped the edge of her plate with his fork. The clink made her blink. Elise forced her mind to refocus. After a second, her senses came back on line. The scent of grilled meat wafted into her airspace. Right. Food. He wanted her to eat something.

Shifting in her chair, Elise stared at her plate. A steak, whole olives stuffed with almonds, and a small mound of corn. Looked good. Picking up her fork, she stabbed an olive. Halfway to her mouth, the sound of footfalls made her pause. She glanced toward the door. Three huge men walked beneath the archway and into the dining room. She froze, watching the group prowl like predators around the table. Plates hit the hideous paisley cloth with a clang. Chairs scraped over the wooden floor.

A large hand slid over her nape.

She jumped in her seat.

"Easy," Cyprus murmured, his grip on her tightening. He pulled her closer. His mouth brushed her ear, helping to relieve some of her tension. "Elise, meet my warriors—Wallaig, Levin and Kruger."

She paid attention, nodding as Cyprus pointed at each one with his knife.

Black-haired and green-eyed, Kruger tipped his chin.

"Greetings, female," Levin murmured, tiger gold gaze leveled on her. "Welcome."

"Thank you," she said, shuffling closer to Cyprus before she turned toward the third man and...lost her ability to breathe. A ginger with gorgeous red hair and a cold expression on his face. Unsmiling. Intense. A badass, and if she were to guess, mean as hell too. But what arrested her attention more than the lethal vibe he projected was his eyes. Cloudy white irises, damaged pupils, one hundred percent blind. Not that she would mention it to the brutal looking warrior. Somehow, she didn't think pointing out his deformity would go over well. Swallowing her fear, she murmured in greeting. "Good to meet you all."

The ginger-haired man growled.

Cyprus shifted in his chair. "Wallaig—fuck off. Stop scaring my female."

One corner of Wallaig's mouth turned up. "Yer a spoilsport, lad. No fun at all."

"Pay him no mind, Elise, he's an arsehole," Cyprus said, amusement in his voice. "And donnae worry about offending him either. Wallaig might be blind, but he sees just fine."

Elise stared at Cyprus a second before curiosity got the best of her. She returned her attention to his warrior. "Seriously? How is that possible?"

"She's a brave one, Cy, I'll grant ye that." With a sigh, pretending her question annoyed him, Wallaig pulled a chair out and sat down on the other side of the table, directly across from her. "'Tis simple enough, lass. Cyprus explained the energy exchange to you, aye?"

Popping the olive in her mouth, she chewed. "Yes."

"So, it's like this—my eyes may be damaged, but I perceive energy on an infinitesimal scale. 'Tis a talent of mine, one I've cultivated over centuries," he said, making it sound normal. More questions popped into her head. She opened her mouth to ask. Wallaig waved his hand, stopping her mid-volley. "Everything

—alive or dead, person, place or thing—possesses an energy signature, one unique unto itself. I may not know what you look like, Elise, but I can read your energy. You've a lovely shape, a beautiful violet tinge to your aura."

Interesting and odd. Titling her head, she met Wallaig's gaze. He looked right at her, as though he really could see her. Her focus ping-ponged, landing on each man, cataloging their differences, before she turned back to Cyprus.

He raised a brow. "Clearer now?"

Yes and no. She pursed her lips. Perhaps a little, but...

"You realize you're all full of..." She paused, struggling to find the right word. Finally, she settled on, "Weirdness."

Levin and Kruger laughed.

Wallaig rolled his damaged eyes.

Cyprus grinned. "And what's your weirdness, lass?"

"Books," she said, happiness sparking to life. Books, books...God, how she loved books. "Rare ones."

Cyprus's focus sharpened on her. "You collect them?"

"I curate and repair them."

"Interesting," Wallaig said, speculation on his face. "What do you do for a living, Elise?"

"I'm a book conservator at the National Museum of Scotland." She frowned, her joy tarnished by the thought of her job. "At least, I used to be."

Murmuring in sympathy, Cyprus wrapped his arms around her. "Take heart, *talmina*. I have something better than a museum for you."

Elise glanced up at him, her expression skeptical. "Better than a museum?"

"A hundred times better."

A thrill shot through her. "What is it?"

"I'll show you when we get home." A devilish gleam in his eyes, he kissed the tip of her nose and let her go. "Now, finish your meal. It's almost time tae go."

Go? To a place better than a museum?

Picking up her knife, Elise dug in, slicing off a piece of steak, wondering at the possibilities. Something better than a *museum*. Oh, boy. Count her in. Label her eager, and as she daydreamed about rare book collections and dragon lairs, Elise realized something odd. Something important. Something just the tiniest bit crazy. She wasn't afraid of what Cyprus planned. Or the lethal-looking dragon guys sitting across the table. Somehow, it all made sense. She fit here, belonged next to Cyprus, was comfortable surrounded by his pack.

What that said about her, Elise didn't know, but chose to ignore the revelation. For now. Later would be soon enough to figure things out and decide what to do: accept her fate or find a way to stay safe, despite the threat, and leave Dragonkind—along with Cyprus—behind.

13

Wings spread wide, Cyprus rocketed between two cliffs. White jets whistled from the tip of his bladed tail. Snow kicked in his wake, whirling between the rise and fall of mountain peaks. Perched on his shoulders, a death grip on the spikes behind his horns, Elise whooped in enjoyment. Concerned for her comfort, he rechecked the harness. All good. Naught for him to worry about. The magical tethers he controlled were doing their job, strapping her in, ensuring her wellbeing, protecting her from taking a tumble. His fire dragon saw to the rest, shielding her from the wind chill, keeping her warm and snug atop his back.

Glancing over his shoulder, he smiled, showing fang. She grinned in return and—

He faked left and flew right, banking around another corner.

Delight in her eyes, she angled her shoulders and leaned into the turn. With a chuckle, he flipped up and over, jetting between two jagged peaks. Elise stayed with him, following each shift as though she'd been born to fly. His heard thumped hard. Goddess, she was beautiful—adventurous and fun, as brave as she was intelligent. A perfect combination that filled his heart so full he wanted to give her more of a ride, but a delay in reaching Cairngorm wouldn't be wise.

Night had fallen, and along with it, the potential for danger.

Grizgunn wouldn't waste any time. He and his pack would be out hunting, in search of the high-energy female that got away. The strength of Elise's bioenergy ensured it. She was a heady lure. One his enemies wouldn't be able to ignore...or resist tracking. The fact he'd wounded Grizgunn's pride by taking Elise fueled the fire, creating the perfect storm. Revenge and desire: a lethal combination in a male as unbalanced as Grizgunn.

Cyprus could smell the challenge in the air. The acrid scent of another warrior lost to a killing rage. So...

No question. The bastard would come.

The only thing left to do now was predict when and where Grizgunn would strike.

Clenching his teeth, Cyprus increased his wing speed. He needed to reach his mountain lair. The sooner he secured Elise inside—behind the magical shield that prevented detection from the outside world—the better. He needed to plot his next move and decide how best to deal with the enemy pack in his territory. Grizgunn required killing, but...his eyes narrowed...how to do it without revealing the reason behind the bastard's obsession with the Scottish pack.

Cyprus frowned. A myriad of options spiraled though his mind, whipping his thoughts into a chaotic jumble. He shook his head. His scales clicked and... shite. Mayhap he was going about it wrong. Mayhap covering up the past—his mistake along with his sire's treachery—wasn't the best thing to do. Mayhap, he should tell his warriors the truth. Reveal all. Tell them everything. Lay what happened the night his sire died at his pack's feet and let the chips fall where they may.

Unease snaked through him.

Telling the truth might well cost him leadership of the Scottish pack. The warriors under his command valued honor, upheld justice and the dictates of Dragonkind. What he'd done landed on the wrong side of the law. Males had been stripped of status and exiled from their homes—even executed—for lesser crimes, but...

Wallaig already knew.

The cunning male hadn't said anything, but he *knew*. Cyprus sensed the weight of his censure, and yet felt Wallaig's approval too. An odd contradiction. One that didn't make him confident about the outcome of unburdening his heart and baring his soul. The inherent vulnerability rubbed him the wrong way, but... such was life. Which meant he must decide—continue to carry the burden alone or trust his brothers-in-arms to have his back when he came clean and confessed his sin.

A dilemma. A dangerous one worth considering, but not right now.

He couldn't think with Elise in the open. Couldn't get past the territorial beast raging inside him. His female sidelined logic, pushing him beyond reason into the primal need to protect.

Urgency whipping at his tail, Cyprus flew around the last bend. Cairngorm rose like a horned monster in front of him. Inhospitable. Unruly. Unpredictable. All teeth and no compassion—a safe haven from the human world, the place he came back to time and again. A home he hoped to share with Elise, if he could convince her to stay.

Scanning the craggy face of the mountain, Cyprus spotted the landing zone. He zeroed in and spread his wings, slowing his flight. An updraft lifted his bulk. He floated above the ledge a moment, seesawing in the wind before his back paws touched down. His claws scraped across granite. His forepaws thumped down. Elise gasped as he reached up, grabbed hold, and lifted her off his back.

As her feet met the ground, he shifted, moving from dragon to human form, and conjured his clothes.

"Oh my God, that was awesome!" With an exuberant hop, she grabbed hold of his shirt front. Blue eyes shining with excitement, she grinned at him. "Can we go again?"

He laughed. "Aye, but not tonight."

Her smile dimmed. "It's not safe?"

"Not yet, but donnae worry, *talmina*." Wrapping his arms around her, he pressed a kiss to her temple. "Grizgunn won't find you here."

"You're sure?"

"Aye," he murmured, hugging her tighter. "The lair is surrounded by a protection spell. Only pack members may enter."

"Oh, okay." Exhaling, she relaxed against him and looked around, examining the rocky ledge. Wide enough to launch three dragons at a time, the outcropping served as a perfect LZ, and one of many entrances and exits into and out of his mountain home. "So, what now?"

"I give you a tour..." Turning toward the doorway cloaked by magic, he grabbed her hand and glanced over his shoulder. Red scales flashing in the gloom, Wallaig lined up his approach. Behind him, Levin and Kruger leveled out, planning to land on either side of the big male. His mouth curved. Time to get out of the way and inside the lair, before his warriors turned them into bowling pins. "And show you you're surprise."

Elise bounced on her toes. "My surprise first, please."

"Impatient lass."

"You probably should get used to that," she said, following him across the landing. "I don't have any."

"What—patience?"

Lacing her fingers with his, she shrugged. "The first flaw of many, I'm afraid."

Cyprus snorted. "Not much of one."

"You're biased."

"Absolutely."

She rolled her eyes.

Cyprus leaned down and pressed a kiss to her lips. A quick brush of his mouth over hers, the delicious taste of her just enough to appease his dragon half and keep his baser instincts in check. A good thing too. He wanted her so much he struggled to maintain his composure. A new state of being for him. He never lost control, in or out of bed. Females came and went, a pleasurable pursuit he forgot about the second he left his bedmate of the moment behind. Elise was different. His reaction to her didn't play by the rules. He craved her with a passion that surpassed natural boundaries. Now, all he could think about was her.

He needed to strip her bare...again. This time, though, it wouldn't be to heal her. He'd take what he wanted: love her so long and hard she sobbed his name as she came.

Unable to resist, he kissed her again. Deeper. Harder. Giving her his tongue before raising his head. As she sputtered in surprise, he banged on the door, requesting entrance into the lair. The beast in control of the spell acquiesced, cracking the portal open without complaint.

"Come, lass." With a gentle tug, he drew her with him, stepped over the threshold, and into the subterranean tunnel. "Your surprise awaits."

Warm air rushed in to surround him as he turned into the first tunnel.

The scrape of dragon claws on stone sounded behind him.

Cyprus didn't wait for his warriors to catch up. He had things to do and a gorgeous female to seduce...to love and hold and cherish. Hopefully, the gift he planned to give her would do the trick. Or at least, nudge Elise in the right direction, toward hot lust and the beginnings of trust. The kind that would allow him his way and land her in the middle his bed.

Manipulative? A wee bit dishonest?

No doubt, but desperate times called for underhanded measures. It might not be honorable, but Cyprus didn't care. With his dragon half in thrall, he couldn't wait to lay her down. She was the blood in his veins and the beat of his heart, the entire reason he existed now. And like it or nay, a male did whatever it took to win his mate. Fair means or foul, the method didn't matter just as long as she accepted his claim, and he got what he needed in the end.

14

One step behind Cyprus, Elise entered the tunnel...then wished she hadn't. Her hand trembled in his as she wrapped her other one around his forearm. Hard muscles flexed against her palm. She took a breath, trying not to panic, and pressed closer. Holy crap, she couldn't see a thing, the blackness so thick it reminded her of the bottomless well.

Deep. Dark. Deadly.

Her imagination worked on her, making her picture awful things. Flexing her fingers, she clung to Cyprus, relying on him to keep her safe and sure footed in the dark.

The ground dipped beneath her feet. She started to shake.

Squeezing her hand, Cyprus murmured a reassurance.

The sound of his voice helped her stay on task. Bend knee. Lift foot. Step forward. The instructions ran like tickertape inside her mind as she shadowed his movements and prayed for light. Silly. Completely ridiculous. Nothing would hurt her as long as she stuck with Cyprus, but...God. She hated the dark. A juvenile fear, one sparked as a child when her father refused to change the bulb in her burnt out nightlight. Her first night without it hadn't been fun, and as much as she tried to reason with herself, unease still dogged her at night. Add in the memory of Grizgunn's attack and—

"Elise?"

"Yeah?"

"Relax, baby. No need tae worry. I can see in the dark."

"Lovely," she said, straining for polite. She didn't make it. An edge crept into her voice, replacing civility with snark. "I'm so happy for you."

He snorted in amusement. "Trouble in a pretty wee package, aren't you, lass? I seem tae remember calling you that earlier this evening."

"You can call me whatever you like, as long as you turn the lights on."

"There aren't any lights in this section of tunnel, but soon we'll be—ah, here we go."

A glow bloomed ahead, growing brighter by the second.

Elise forced herself to breathe. In. Out. Fill her lungs. Release the air. Step through an archway behind Cyprus and...there, all better. Lots of light. Enough to get a sense of the underground tunnel and see where she stood. Or rather, walked beside him. He led. She followed, wide-eyed now, her head on a swivel, cataloging everything about the place Cyprus called home.

Smooth, well-worn stone floors. High vaulted ceilings supported by granite half-columns embedded in curved walls. Following the chisel marks, she glanced up and...wow. Hundreds of round lanterns, big and small, glowing softly, bobbing like jellyfish against the arched roof. Elise frowned at the strange lamp colony. Weird. She couldn't see any electrical cables or connections. She examined the globes more closely and... nope. Not a single power outlet in sight.

Looking ahead, she watched the light-filled orbs sway, then nudged Cyprus with her elbow. "Does the lair run on magic?"

"This one does, aye."

This one? Did that mean...

"You have another lair?"

"One in the city, in the center of Aberdeen, beneath the pub we own." Cyprus turned down another corridor. Wider than the last, the tunnel stretched out before them, then branched in two different directions. "But I've always preferred the mountain lair."

"And the other warriors?"

"Most sleep here. Rannock spends his days in the city. You've yet tae meet him, but he runs the whiskey distillery behind the pub," he said. "Tydrin—my blood brother—splits his times between here and there. Ivy prefers the city. She enjoys walking to the market and visiting the shops during daylight hours."

She glanced at him in surprise. "You have a brother?"

"Two, actually. Tydrin is the youngest. Vyroth is my twin."

Her mouth curved. A twin...how cool for Cyprus. As the only child in a dysfunctional household, she imagined how much fun that would've been for him. God knew she'd longed for a sister to play with growing up. "Identical?"

"Aye," he murmured, looking troubled for a moment. "Although, one of his eyes is bright blue."

"What color is the other one?"

"Pale purple—like mine."

"Cool," she said, squeezing his hand, no longer bothered by all the weird dragon information. The more she learned, the more intrigued she became by Cyprus and his family. "And who is Ivy?"

"Tydrin's mate. You'll meet her later. He promised tae fly her out before dawn."

Another woman inside a dragon pack. Thank God. Elise had a feeling she would need a compatriot—a female friend who understood Dragonkind. "Has she been with Tydrin long?"

Cyprus shook his head. "A few months. Tydrin mated her after rescuing her from a FBI manhunt."

"She's a criminal?"

"A fugitive from the United States, until she cleared her name."

Wow. Seriously? Sounded like an interesting story. She started to ask, but got sidetracked as Cyprus walked beneath an open arch. He stopped just inside a huge room. Except...her eyes narrowed on the architecture...it wasn't a room at all. The domed structure looked like a cave. Hewn from black granite, the color palette should've felt oppressive. Somehow, the dark walls managed to convey warmth instead.

The sparkling veins of crystals helped, cutting through black stone, acting like pale paint on an ebony canvas. More light globes hovered near the ceiling, brightening the space, casting long shadows across the floor. Her gaze swung toward a kitchen with Birchwood cabinets and marble countertops. The butcher-block island with backless stools screamed comfortable, homey, lived in: a place where cookies got baked and secrets came to be discovered.

Dragging her attention to the other side of the cavern, Elise tried not to laugh. What she'd expected, she didn't know, but...jeepers. Dragon guys sure lived a lot like human guys. The bachelor pad vibe was a dead giveaway. No frills or throw pillows. No fuzzy blankets. Zero extra comforts. Just long leather couches, low-lying end tables, and a bunch of colorful bean bag chairs. Lips twitching, she scanned the room again and…drat it all. Not a single book in sight.

"The great room, Elise. The pack spends a lot of time in here."

"This isn't my surprise, is it?"

He grinned at her hopeful tone. "Nay, but we must pass through here to get to it. Follow me, *talmina*."

Without waiting for a reply, he drew her forward—crossing the weathered stone floor, detouring around a grand piano, sidestepping a yoga mat—to reach a wide entry way on the other side of the cave. He jogged up the steps. She kept pace, boot soles beating a predictable rhythm, before stepping into a vestibule. Another archway. She caught a glimpse of the room across the foyer

Her heart paused mid-thump. "Is that what I think it is?"

"Go and see, lass."

Shaking free of Cyprus's hand, she headed for the entrance. Her feet took her across the tiled mosaic floor. Elise hardly noticed. She was too busy staring… hoping and praying too. As she paused under the arch, her breath hitched. Wonder filled her. One hand pressed to chest, Elise looked her fill and—

"Holy crap," she whispered, awe in her voice. Books. Thousands of them. Row upon row of tall antique cases pressed end-to-end. Her gaze jumped to the second floor. More of the same, wall-to-wall, paradise clad in Cherrywood. "A library."

"One of the largest in Britain." A step behind her, Cyprus pointed at the spiral staircase leading one level up. "Perhaps not as extensive as the museum's, but close."

"God." Elise shook her head, unable to believe what she was seeing. "All the wood is hard-carved, isn't it?"

"Every molding, banister and bookshelf. My uncle invited a human master craftsmen tae visit in the eighteenth century. He is credited with designing the library."

"Invited?" She huffed, knowing better than that. Dragonkind didn't do things in the usual way. Males of his kind never invite humans *anywhere*, never mind into their homes...unless, of course, the human happened to be female and it couldn't be helped. "Or imprisoned?"

His lips twitched. "Before my time, lass. But from what I understand, Jacob was very happy here."

"I'm sure, but..."

As she trailed off, Cyprus frowned. "What?"

"God, Cyprus." Turning full circle in the center of the room, she stared at the splendor. "Words aren't enough to describe it. It's incredible, the most beautiful library I have ever seen."

"What if I told you it isn't the best part?"

Elise threw him a look of disbelief. *Not the best part?* He'd clearly lost his mind. Nothing came close to the plush reading chairs and velvet upholstered couches. The antique work tables and glass covered cases with antique manuscripts inside weren't sloppy seconds either and—holy crap. She scanned the stacks again. The sheer enormity of it floored her, and the books...God. The *books*, so many beautiful leatherbound books.

"Do you like my gift, Elise?"

"Yes," she said, unable to speak above a whisper.

"Good. Now, come here." He held out his hand. Dragging her gaze from the room, she took it without hesitation, letting him lead her toward a wall clad in wood paneling. He tapped the bronze dragon perched on the center panel. "Press on it."

She held his gaze, then did as he asked and pushed against the emblem. A click sounded. The dragon moved backward, disappearing into the hole left by its absence. Gears ground into motion. A quiet clank. A whirling whisper. The shift of warm air and—

The wall slid sideways to reveal a solid, steel door.

Round instead of square, it looked like a fancy bank vault. Elise studied it, examining the outer edges, searching for seams, looking for a way to open it. No luck. No combination lock, electronic keypad or touch screen either. No handle to turn or button to press, just a seamless steel door with a flat face and no apparent way in.

Glancing over her shoulder, she looked at Cyprus. "What's in there?"

"Place your hand here." Knocking against steel with his knuckle, he indicted the spot and settled behind her. His chest pressed against her back. His breath warmed the side of her neck. His spicy scent rose to surround her. Her body reacted, whipping her hormones into a frenzy, distracting her as he cupped her hand and set it against the vault door. Threading his fingers between hers, he pressed his palm to the back of her hand, leaned in, and murmured in her ear, "Ask it to open, Elise."

With him so close, need sank deep. Her muscles twitched as her mind screamed, wanting her to forget about the vault and pay attention to him. Great idea. Super suggestion, one she needed to follow before—

"Elise—quit teasing me. Do as you are told."

"So bossy," she murmured, squirming against him, struggling to gain control. He rumbled a warning. She swallowed a moan and did as he asked. "Open Sesame."

Cyprus chuckled.

Heat raced across her palm. Steel warmed beneath her skin. A purple glow eclipsed the vault face, spreading out to touch the edges. Elise gasped as something clicked deep inside her, like a key turning in a lock and...

The door cracked opened, then widened, forcing her to step back.

"The vault is magically sealed. It has a mind of its own, but knows you by touch now. Your bio-energy is the key tae unlocking it." Keeping his arms around her, he nipped her ear lobe and, nudging her forward, walked her ahead of him into the vault. "You will be able tae open it any time you like from now on."

Unable to concentrate with his mouth on her skin, she nodded. "Sure. Okay and—oh my God, do that again."

Licking over her pulse point, he smiled against the side of her throat. "Explore first, *talmina*, pleasure second."

She forced her eyes open. Right. No problem. She could do that, explore a little before getting to the good stuff, like—

Her attention landed on a stack of books sitting on a scarred tabletop. She read the first title. Her attention jumped to the second. The third and fourth registered. Her mouth fell open as she stared at the fifth leather-bound spine. She jerked against Cyprus, shifting to take in the entire room.

"Dear God."

A collection of rare books, some of the most coveted on the planet. She scanned title after title. Some she'd read about in museum journals, some she'd seen in pictures and heard about at conferences, but... someone pinch her. Or punch her. She needed to wake up. It couldn't be—just *couldn't*—but as her knees went weak (and Cyprus held her up), Elise knew she wasn't dreaming. It was real. A whole room full of rich and rare finds.

"Cyprus..." she said, struggling to find the right words. "You realize...this is...the value in this room can't be measured. Most of these books are priceless: first additions, the only known copies, like no others in the world."

Hugging her from behind, he rested his chin on top of her head. "I know. And now, all of it...each and every one...belongs tae you."

She swallowed, fighting back tears. Oh, God—the responsibility. The enormity and absolute privilege of curating such a collection. "How can you...would you really trust me with it?"

"My uncle loved books. He spent a great deal of time in here," he said, his gaze skimming over the shelves. "None of my warriors have an interest in his collection. The manuscripts, scrolls, books and treatise haven't been seen tae in years. You're as passionate about books as he was, lass. I can hear it in your voice, see it on your face and..." Cupping her jaw, he tipped her head back, turning her face up to his. The approval in his eyes took her breath away. "I hear it in your heart too, so aye. Of course, I trust you with it. The collection needs your care, Elise. My hope is you will build on what my uncle started, add tae his legacy, and make it your own."

"You...I can't even begin to...you have no idea how

much..." Her throat tightened, cutting off her words. Her dream laid out at her feet, in one room, given to her by a man she'd only just met, yet felt more connected to than people she'd known all her life. He was incredible. Beyond generous. The kind of man she'd always wanted, but hadn't believed existed.

Wiping a tear from her cheek, she turned and laid her hands on his chest. "Hey, Cyprus?"

"Aye, lass?"

"Kiss me."

He sucked in a breath. Heat kindled in his eyes as he dipped his head. "I thought tae give you more time before we—"

"I don't need more time. I need you." Caressing his shoulders, she offered him her mouth. "Please, Cyprus, kiss me."

An impatient request? Too much, too soon? Maybe, but Elise didn't care how crazy it sounded. Or that Cyprus was probably right. She needed to make love with him. He wanted her just as much, so...

To hell with restraint and reason. Forget about playing it safe.

Pressing her body to his, she moaned and sank into the pleasure of his kiss. God, his touch and taste, the way he made her feel: beautiful, passionate, like a colorful bird in a faraway land. She couldn't get enough and didn't try. Elise let go instead, allowed him to control the pace and her pleasure, embracing her bliss, encouraging him to take more. Right now, in this moment, he was all that mattered. She wanted to live and experience. Tomorrow would be soon enough for regret.

15

Elise tasted like an exotic treat. Sweet and spicy, so hot she surpassed needy rocketing straight to naughty. Not that he was complaining. He never imagined she would be like this—all over him, hands and mouth working in tandem, driving him crazy as she learned his body and sucked on his tongue. Fuck. She was his dirtiest dream come true. A goddess come to life. He adored her eagerness. Loved the boldness that shoved her inhibitions aside, pushing him past his own, making him greedy for more of her.

With a hum, he encouraged her to go farther. Touch more. Kiss him harder. Be as aggressive as she wanted.

She tugged at his T-shirt.

He broke the kiss long enough to yank it over his head. She touched him everywhere, chest, shoulders, back, ran her clever fingers across abdomen. The scrape of her nails on his skin made him quiver. Pleasure vaulted into holy fuck territory. His dick jumped behind his button-fly, impatient for her, wanting the same kind of treatment from her hand.

Elise whispered his name. "Kiss me."

Under her spell, Cyprus dipped his head and invaded her mouth. She curled her arms around his neck, tongue dueling with his, and pulled him closer. Hmm, she was delicious. So beautiful in her desire: brazen and unabashed, reckless with demand. And her natural perfume—bloody hell, he could smell her, the sharp pitch of arousal combined with the intoxicating scent of her skin. Beautiful beyond belief, and so potent it made him lightheaded.

Cyprus breathed deep, taking another hit, wanting to lick the fragrance from her skin. He tried to hold back, to slow down and treat her as gently as she deserved.

Fisting her hands in his hair, she nipped his bottom lip. He groaned and kissed her again, losing himself, giving her all she asked.

Goddess, he couldn't get enough.

He wanted more. More of her taste. More of her touch. More of the soft sounds she made as he cupped her arse and pulled her against him. Elise wiggled, adjusting their fit, cradling his erection against the soft curve of her belly. Bloody hell, she unhinged him. Was magic, pure pleasure, a wee temptress with clever hands and a wicked tongue. His equal in every way, and so demanding she launched him into uncharted territory.

A death grip on the urge to forget foreplay and go straight to fucking, Cyprus slipped his hand beneath her oversized sweatshirt. Smooth, warm skin caressed his fingertips. He brushed his hand over her waist, up her back and around her ribcage. She squirmed in his arms. He stroked over her skin with singular purpose, learning her shape, searching for the sensitive spots that would drive her wild.

He wanted her hot and greedy. Slick and ready, so aroused she came at least once before he took her. Twice would be better, but with passion lashing him —and Elise holding the whip—he wouldn't last that long. She threatened his control, rubbing her breasts against his chest, scraping her nails over his scalp, whimpering as though she would perish without his touch.

Cyprus understood her reaction.

With his dragon in full flame, he burned for her, firing so hot his mind shut down. The world ceased to exist. All that mattered was Elise—kissing her, touching her, loving her until she called his name, and he came apart in her arms.

The thought acted like a Molotov cocktail.

A fireball of lust exploded through him.

Cyprus groaned into her mouth. Goddess help him. Not good. He needed to rein himself in right now. Before she drove him over the edge of reason and... aye. Absolutely. Slowing down was a great plan. One in need of immediate implementation. Easier said than done in the arms of a wee temptress with nimble hands tugging the buttons of his fly open.

Warm fingers wrapped around his erection.

Pleasure weakened his knees. Cyprus wrenched his mouth from hers. "Bloody hell, lass."

Denied his kiss, Elise licked over his pulse point. Wet tongue on his skin. Busy hand down the front of his jeans and...oh fuck. She felt so good. Hot palm. Firm grip. Rhythm just right as she stroked him root to tip. The muscles roping his abdomen tightened. Each breath coming hard, his hips followed each caress, begging for more of her touch. Unable to stop himself, Cyprus tipped his head back and let Elise have her way, groaning with each slow pump. The pad of her thumb circled the head of his cock, caressed the sensitive underside, driving him closer to madness with every tantalizing glide.

Her fingers pulsed around him. Once. Twice. A third time...

His chest heaved. "Holy fuck, Elise."

"Feel good?"

"Aye, but..." He cursed as she stoked him again. Harder. A wee bit faster, demolishing his control. "You need tae stop now. I won't last if you—"

"I need a taste, Cyprus," she whispered, nipping his skin.

A taste. His brow furrowed. Of him? Cyprus opened his eyes. Not understanding, he stared down at her. Lowering her mouth to his chest, she swirled her tongue around his nipple. The sensitive nub contracted, sending bliss in a straight line to his balls.

"Please?" Pretty blue eyes peeked up at him.

Locked in a carnal fog, he blinked, trying to make sense of her request. Elise flicked him with her tongue again. He drew in a deep breath. Was she asking if she could...if he would let her...

His brain turned over. Understanding struck, hitting him like a lightning bolt. Cyprus exhaled hard. Oh, man. Only an idiot would say no. He craved the pleasure she would give him more than his next breath, but...he frowned. Elise was his mate. His to protect, nurture and please. He didn't want her doing anything that made her uncomfortable.

The idea cooled his ardor in a hurry. Thank the goddess. It was about time his brain started working and his cock stopped calling the shots.

Cupping her chin, he forced her to look at him. "You wish tae pleasure me with your mouth?"

She blushed, but nodded.

"Do you enjoy giving head, Elise?"

"I don't know. I've never tried it, but I want to with you," she said, honest desire in her voice, the need to please in her eyes. "Give me a taste, Cyprus. Just a little one. You can do whatever you want to me, afterward."

Her *'whatever you want'* got him moving.

His nostrils flared. A plan formed. Stepping back, he looked her over. "Clothes off, *talmina*. I want you naked and kneeling when you use that gorgeous mouth on me."

Shock flared in her eyes. She hesitated, her hands fisted in the front of her sweatshirt. A moment passed before she pulled it up, exposing the enticing curve of her belly. She revealed her breasts next, making his mouth water as she tugged the sweater over her head. Blonde hair in a tumble around her shoulders, she pushed jogging pants over her hips. Arousal spiked in her scent as she bared her body, telling him he was on the right path. Elise might not be accustomed to taking orders in bed, but she would take them from him. He ruled in the bedroom and, despite the chaotic beginning to their coupling, she needed to know he would take control of her passion and reward her with pleasure.

Kicking out of her pants, she stood proud, offering herself, humbling him.

His shaft kicked as he looked her over. Pale skin. Pink lips. Full breasts with tightly furled nipples. A small waist that curved into lush hips and a round arse he longed to get his hands on again. But he would wait—give her all the time she needed—before paying homage. Before worshiping every hill and valley, every inch of her sweet-smelling skin.

"Beautiful, Elise." Trapping her gaze with his, he held out his hand. "Come here."

Her fingers slid across his palm.

He conjured a thick pillow and, setting it at his feet, widened his button-fly. "On your knees, *talmina*."

Excitement flushed her cheeks as she kneeled in front of him. Shifting on the cushion, she gazed at his erection and raised her hand. Her fingertips touched down, skated along his length, making his muscles tighten, and him pray for mercy. Elise showed him none. She wet her lips instead, making him groan, and leaned forward. The tip of her nose touched his shaft. Bliss whispered his name as she breathed deep, scenting him and—

Her soft mouth brushed over him. "Hmm, you taste good."

The comment made him pulse with anticipation.

He clenched his teeth, clinging to control, determined to hang on, loving the sight of her at his feet. Unable to look away, he watched and felt and...nearly died when she swirled her tongue over the head of his cock. His heart jackhammered the inside of his chest. His breathing went haywire as she opened her mouth and pushed forward, engulfing him in soft, steamy heat.

Delight poured into his veins.

A raw sound left his throat and...goddess almighty. Jesus fucking Christ. The heat, the scorching pleasure, twisted him through him. Volcanic need boiled over. He wanted inside her, wasn't going to last, but holy hell...he planned to try. His female wanted the experience. Had asked so beautifully, needing to please him as much as he wanted to pleasure her. He saw her enthusiasm as he fisted one of his hands in her hair, felt her enjoyment with each sucking pull around his shaft, so...aye. He would stand strong, hold on, and let her have her way. Even if ecstasy brought him to his knees, and he lost his mind in the end.

16

Anyone who thought a woman couldn't be powerful while on her knees was wrong. Dead *wrong*. The belief must be a myth. A trumped-up misconception, but Elise knew better now. Blowjobs equaled power, on a grand scale. The kind every woman ought to wield, and as she swirled her tongue around Cyprus, learning what he liked, holding him in thrall with her mouth, she wondered what the hell had taken her so long. She should have been more adventurous and tried it sooner. Then again, maybe not.

Maybe wanting sex this way depended on the man. Maybe she wouldn't have enjoyed it with someone else. No one but Cyprus had ever made her feel desired and cherished, needed and important, as though she was somehow vital to him.

With a purr of enjoyment, she bobbed up to suck on the tip of his erection. He groaned. She slid back down. His hand tightened in her hair. She did it again, shaking his foundation, increasing his pleasure, making him a prisoner of her desire.

God, she loved the taste of him. Loved feeling his muscles flex and release. Adored hearing his rough growls and guttural groans. Relished driving him to the edge of control and keeping him there. She hummed again. Soon, any second now...

She opened wider, taking more of him. Another quick flick over the sensitive spot she discovered beneath the head, and he'd lose—

"Bloody hell, lass. Not so fast." Fisting her hair, he slowed her strokes, fighting his need to come.

Satisfaction whipped through her. He was close. So very close, and she was the cause. Was about to demolish his control and push him over the edge. She sucked harder.

He cursed under his breath. "Use your tongue, *talmina*. Take me deeper."

Letting him guide her, she obeyed and opened wider, welcoming him and all he gave her. Her head bobbed as her tongue swirled, licking over his length. She took him to the back of her throat with the next stroke.

"Goddess," he rasped, fingers gripping her hair, his eyes on her face. "That's it, Elise. Give me more and... goddamn, you feel good. So fucking good."

He increased the rhythm, giving her more to swallow.

She egged him on, so aroused she ached inside. An orgasm hung on the horizon, in view but out of reach and...hmm, baby. She needed it. Wanted to come so badly she hurt. With a whimper, Elise pressed her knees together, searching for relief and—

"No more. I cannae wait any longer."

Drawing her mouth away, Cyprus lifted and spun her around. Her toes brushed the floor a second before he pivoted toward the table. Shoving books out of the way, he curled his hand over her shoulder and bent her forward. Her belly met the tabletop. The balls of her feet balanced on the floor, a tremor of excitement rumbled through her. She was at his mercy. Ass in the air, breasts pressed to the wooden surface, zero ability to move. Elise shivered in anticipation. He kicked her legs apart and stepped between her feet. The warmth of his chest brushed her spine as he pinned her down and stroked through her folds.

"You're ready," he said, his breath hot in her ear. A blunt finger touched her clit. Slick with arousal, he drew excruciating circles around the sensitive bundle, playing, teasing, driving her to the brink of ecstasy. "So hot, Elise. So wet. You enjoyed sucking my cock, dinnae you?"

Dirty words. Instant arousal and...God, had she ever. She tried to answer. Nothing but breathy gasps came out.

"Tell me true, lass." Pushing two fingers inside her, he stroked gently.

In. Out. Rub a spot deep inside her and retreat. Sharp pleasure bloomed.

Swallowing, she worked moisture back into her mouth. "Yes."

"You want me tae fuck you now?"

Tilting her hips into his touch, she whimpered.

"Answer me." His fingers paused, withholding her orgasm.

"Yes! Oh God, please. Please, Cyprus."

He growled in approval. "Hold on tight, *talmina*. Your first ride is going tae be a rough one."

The threat lit her up. Heat pooled in her abdomen. Rough. Gentle. Up against the wall or face down on a table. Elise didn't care. The position didn't matter just as long as he kept his promise and took her hard.

She moaned as his fingers left her.

He came right back and, positioning himself,

pressed in. Her back arched. He pushed her back onto the tabletop. Holding her down, restraining her movement, Cyprus forged forward, filling her so full she clenched around him. Bliss exploded outward. Bright light flashed behind her eyelids. She heard him snarl. Felt his teeth scrap her shoulder as he set a quick pace, hammering into her from behind. Hard and fast. Rough and delicious. Over and over. She came again, pulsing around him as Cyprus used her for his pleasure, took what he needed, and shouted her name.

17

S tanding at the foot of the bed, Cyprus watched
his mate sleep. Candlelight from the ensuite
bath spilled into his bedroom, flickering across
stone floors and curved walls, anointing her with
golden light. Not that he needed it to see her. Night
vision pinpoint sharp, he saw every detail: the soft
turn of her pale cheek, the messy tumble of her blond
hair, the tilt of full lips still swollen from his kisses.

Satisfaction welled inside him. Goddess, she was
adorable.

On her back, arms flung wide, legs askew beneath
the sheet, Elise slept the same way she made love—
with complete abandon. Nothing held back. No shy-
ness to be seen. Just a gorgeous female in repose, totally exhausted after spending a full night and day
with him. Time well spent. Gratification guaranteed.
His mouth curved. He hadn't left her alone. Hell, he
hadn't been able to, making love to her over and over,
delving between her thighs so many times her taste
was now imprinted on his heart.

Buckling his belt, Cyprus touched his tongue to
his bottom lip. Fuck, he could still taste her. Wanted to
strip away the sheets and lick her until she screamed

again. Temptation stampeded his willpower. His body reacted, hardening behind his button-fly. With a growl, he stepped around the corner of the bed and—

Cyprus shook his head. Nay, not again.

Planting his feet, he held himself in check. Perfectly fucking still. He needed to get a grip on his urges before he took another step...and did something foolish. He might be ready for another round, but Elise wasn't in any shape to take him. She required time to recover, to rest muscles he knew must be sore as a result of his insatiability.

Not that she'd been any better.

He could still hear her breathy moans. Still felt her slick heat surrounding him. The memory of her under —and over—him turned him inside out. She'd ridden him like she owned him the last time, as though she ruled, leaving him to follow. He huffed in amusement. Such a bold lass. So beautiful she made him want to pull his clothes off and crawl back into bed with her. Again.

Too bad he couldn't stay. Not tonight.

Cyprus backed away from the edge of the bed. His gaze landed on the covered tray he'd left for her. It wasn't much, a couple of croissants, some berries, sliced cheese along with an energy drink, but it would do...for now. Until he returned from a night hunting Grizgunn and fed her himself.

With a sigh of regret, he headed for the door. Footfalls muffled by thick area rugs, Cyprus crossed the open space, mind churning, worry rising as he sensed his brothers-in-arms presence inside the lair. Already gathered in the great room, prowling around like a pack of wild dogs, his warriors awaited him, thoughts of killing rogue males on their minds.

Even from across the lair, he felt the tension. The

threat of violence churned in the air, broadcasting the lethal slant of each warrior's mood.

Cyprus grunted. On a normal night, he would've approved, but...shite. Tonight promised to be anything but *normal*. Clusterfuck might be a better word to use. Deadly was no doubt another, but—no help for it. He couldn't stall any longer. The truth needed to be told and past sins uncovered.

With his mate now in play, he stood at a fork in the road. Turn right or go left. Keep his secret or choose a healthier way forward: a future for himself and Elise without the threat of discovery hanging over his head, without his past tainting everything it touched. Cyprus knew coming clean was the right thing to do. Felt it deep down. Had known it for years, but the uncertainty of his warriors' reaction had kept him silent.

Hell, it still worried him. Unease picked him apart as he tried to anticipate what his brothers-in-arms would say. He frowned. How would they react to his confession—with understanding or censure? With calm acceptance or gut-wrenching violence? Cyprus swallowed past the tightness in his throat. It could go either way. The males he commanded were honorable, so strong none backed away from a challenge. Or allowed dishonesty to stand. A tight spot to be in considering the lass asleep in his bed.

Concern formed a knot in the center of his chest.

Goddess help him...Elise. She was part of his mess now too. His female would be affected by his decision. She could be hurt by what happened next and—

Fucking hell. He'd only just found her. Didn't want to leave her. Would end his own life before harming a single hair on her head, but the fact remained. His warriors held the power to condemn him. He'd committed a cardinal sin that night—executing his sire without pack approval. Aye, he'd had good reason. The law actually stood on his side given the foul nature of his father's crime. His uncle and cousins lay dead, ashes scattered across highland moors, the horror of it his sire's doing.

Cyprus flexed his hand around the door handle. The metal knob crumbled in his palm as he shook his head. He must accept responsibility for his part in it. Laying the blame at his da's feet didn't exonerate him. Or excuse his actions. Sometimes doing the right thing wasn't always the best thing. Which meant...

Time to face the music.

Pulling in another deep breath, Cyprus opened the door and slipped into the hallway. Careful to be quiet, not wanting to wake Elise, he pulled it closed behind him. The lock clicked into place. He raised his head and—

Stopped short.

Dark purple eyes narrowed on him. "About time you got yer sorry arse out of bed."

Cyprus snorted. "Fuck off, Tydrin. You're no better. I can smell Ivy all over you."

Arms crossed, leaning against the wall opposite the door, his brother grinned. "She's not up yet. Won't be for a while."

"Elise, either," he said, pride for his mate rising. "I wore her out."

"Good for you." A knowing gleam in his eyes, Tydrin pushed away from the wall. An inch shorter and less broad of shoulder, his brother raised his fist and thumped Cyprus on the chest. The love-tap resonated, pushing through to the back of his spine. "Better for her."

"Shite, I hope so." He might be newly mated, but Cyprus wasn't stupid. He knew where his priorities lay, and pleasing his female topped the list. "There a reason you're out here waiting for me? Or are you just being annoying."

"I live to annoy you."

"That's because you're an arsehole," he said, affection in his tone.

Tydrin chuckled.

Cyprus pivoted right, leaving his doorway to stride down the hallway. Light globes reacted to the shift, bobbing against the ceiling, highlighting the chisel marks in ancient stone walls. Hundreds of years old, the lair settled around him like a favorite pair of jeans. Well-loved. Worn in spots, comfortable despite its age. Rolling his shoulders, he let his home soothe the ragged edges of worry as his brother kept pace, walking alongside him. Silence stretched, nothing but the sound of boot soles striking stone in the underground tunnel.

Minutes passed before he threw Tydrin a sidelong look. Odd. His brother wasn't usually so quiet. The change in behavior signaled trouble, the kind Cyprus refused to ignore.

Slowing the pace, he nudged Tydrin with his elbow. "What?"

His brows furrowed, his brother met his gaze. "Something's wrong."

"What do you mean?"

"With you. Something is wrong with you."

Cyprus scowled. Perceptive wee runt, wasn't he? To be expected. He couldn't hide much from Tydrin. As blood brothers, their connection ran deeper than pack bonds, tying thoughts and emotions together, allowing him to sense Tydrin and Vyroth's moods...even when he wasn't with them. A gift, most of the time. Tonight, though, he wished the link wasn't so strong. It might've saved Tydrin some heartache.

"I'm all right, lad."

"You're unsettled, Cy. I feel it...can sense yer struggle with every breath I take. And now you've called a formal meeting of the pack, which you never do." Gaze intent on him, Tydrin scanned his face. "What worries you, brother?"

"Grizgunn—"

"Nay, donnae lie. Not to me. 'Tis more than the thought of a feud. We've had rogues in our territory before without it unsettling you."

His feet slowed. He halted in the middle of an intersection. Four tunnels converged, then spiraled in different directions. Cyprus stared straight ahead, seeing the hallway in front of him, but not really. Time to decide. What should he do? Tell his brother, or wait to confess in front of the entire pack. Indecision warred, pitting fear against courage.

Bowing his head, Cyprus cupped the nape of his neck with both hands. "Fuck."

"It cannae be that bad, brother."

"It is that bad, Tydrin."

"Then tell me," he said from right behind him. "So, we can fix it."

"It cannae be fixed." Guilt rose, clogging his throat. "Or undone."

Grabbing his shoulder, Tydrin spun him around. "Tell me."

He met his brother's gaze. Son of a bitch. It should never have come to this. He wanted to protect Tydrin. The eldest shielded the youngest, only natural, but... goddess forgive him. He couldn't shield his brother from the truth, from a secret so devastating it held the power to shatter his pack.

Which meant Tydrin must be told first.

Blindsiding him in front of the other warriors wasn't a good idea. His brother might be smart, but he owned a temper. An explosive one that, once unleashed, needed time to cool. Tydrin deserved more than silence from him. He needed the truth before anyone else heard it. Anything less would be cruel. The betraying bastard had been his sire too, after all, so...

Cyprus nodded. "It has tae do with Father and the night he died."

"What about it?"

"I am responsible for his death," he said, his voice cracking. Christ, it sounded bad when said out loud, something he'd never dared do before now. "He orchestrated the ambush that killed our uncle and cousins."

Tydrin flinched and stepped back, away from him. "What the fuck are you talking about?"

The question opened the floodgates. The truth spilled out in a messy rush.

"He was in league with Rodin and the Archguard, Tydrin," he rasped, tasting bile as he tried to control the volatile swirl of his emotions. "Father believed he'd been chosen tae rule by the Goddess of All Things...that command, position, and privilege had been stolen from him. After the ambush, the pack was in turmoil. The chaos was absolute and—"

"I remember," Tydrin whispered, looking as pale as he felt. "I was in the kitchen with Aunt Vivian when she collapsed."

And died.

Tydrin refused to say it. He didn't want to either, but the harshness didn't make it any less true. The instant his uncle—her mate—had drawn his last breath, she had too.

Raking his fingers through his hair, Cyprus drew a shaky breath. "I went tae find Da, hoping he would know what tae do. I found him with Randor—Grizgunn's sire—on a hill above the battlefield. He'd watched it all. Watched our kin and commander be slaughtered and did naught tae stop it. When he saw me, he laughed...he fucking *laughed*, Tydrin. Was so pleased, he boasted how well his plan had worked and—"

"You lost your temper."

Shite. If only he had. If only he could use loss of control as an excuse, but...

"I cannae claim anger as a defense," he said, being honest, refusing to hide anymore. "I knew what I was doing when I chased him down. I showed no mercy. I executed him with a clear mind and a vengeful heart. His blood is on my claws, brother."

His words hung in the air.

Cyprus closed his eyes. He couldn't look at his brother. Couldn't bear to see—

The fist caught him on the cheekbone.

His head snapped to the side. Blood splattered over his temple as he stumbled backward. His spine collided with the wall. The pain hammered him next, exploding between his temples, rattling his teeth, piercing his heart. Fucking hell, his brother knew how to hit. Packed one hell of a wallop in a knuckle sized package. And as Tydrin hit him again, catching him under the chin, Cyprus snarled but stood firm, refusing to fight back. He deserved to be punished. Deserved each punch Tydrin threw, but as he braced for the next, something odd happened.

Tydrin stepped back, denying him the third strike.

"There. I have drawn first blood and taken my due. *Grevaiz* has been accepted and satisfied, commander."

Flinching in a surprise, Cyprus regained his balance and looked at his brother. *Grevaiz*, the settling of accounts between warriors. An ancient Dragonkind ritual, the offering of first strike when one male wronged another. A way for the offended to be assuaged and the offender to be forgiven. Cyprus exhaled, the sound rough and raw. Jesus. Leave it to Tydrin to trot out tradition in the face of overwhelming emotion.

Tears stinging his eyes, he stared at his brother, wonder spinning him toward gratitude.

"It's over, Cyprus." An unyielding look in his face, Tydrin met him head-on, all warrior, no sign of sympathy. "You are forgiven."

Relief nearly brought him to his knees. "I thought you would hate me."

"You thought wrong," he said. "I was there too, you know. I am not blind. Father was mentally ill, Cyprus...so mad near the end, his part in our kin's murders doesn't surprise me. You did what needed to be done, sparing the rest of us the pain of it. That takes strength and courage, brother...is the entire reason you were chosen to lead our pack after Uncle's death."

"But—"

His brother snarled at him. "How many times did you shield me from da growing up, Cy? How many times did you step between us? How many times did you protect me when I couldn't protect myself?"

The memories slammed into him like surging waves. All the verbal abuse. All the raised fists. Every bruise meted out in anger. "Tae many too count."

"Well, now it's my turn to shield you. I will stand

beside you when you tell the pack what you just told me. I have yer back, brother, and always will." Stepping in close, Tydrin gripped his nape. Dark purple gaze aglow, he held him steady, then gave him a little shake. "Never forget it."

Not knowing what to say, Cyprus palmed his brother's shoulder. He squeezed. His brother accepted the unspoken thank you, standing chest-to-chest with him as the bonds of brotherhood snapped back into place. All good. The past out in the open, and his brother on board. Now, to face the rest of his pack.

Drawing a deep breath, he patted Tydrin again, love and affection in the touch, and released his hold. His brother reciprocated and drew back, giving him space to turn and continue down the corridor. True to his word, Tydrin matched him stride for stride, walking shoulder-to-shoulder with him toward the great room where his warriors—and fate—awaited.

18

C yprus bit down on a groan as he hit the ground. Pressing his palm to pitted stone, his muscles shook as he tried to push upright. Made by dragon claws, deep gouges on the surface of the LZ scored his skin. Another round of pain streaked through him. Chest heaving, he struggled to regain his feet. Howling winter wind blew into the wide opening between the jagged snarl of towering rock. The cold raked over his bare skin, chilling the blood on his back, urging him to turn belly up and cry mercy.

Blinking red ooze from his eyes, he shook his head to clear his vision. *Cry mercy*, his arse. Staying down wasn't a good idea. He needed to get back on his feet. The next strike would come any moment, but—

Goddamn. He hurt all over.

His brothers-in-arms showed no leniency. Little compassion either. Cyprus breathed through the agony. Shite. The males didn't know the meaning of the word. Each stood strong, adhering not only to tra- dition, but the spirit of *grevaiz*. A necessary thing. After coming clean and telling his warriors all, he wanted the punishment. Needed the censure to strip away the past. To assuage his guilt. To carve away the bitterness and allow him to feel clean again. Had the pack gone lightly—and shown mercy—he would never have felt their forgiveness.

So, he endured. Strike after strike. Brutal knuckles and hard hits. Being knocked down again and again... without lifting a finger to protect himself.

Bloodied and bruised, aching all over, he rolled onto his arse. Blood dripped into his eyes but not before he saw a pair of boots stop beside him. A hand appeared in front of his face. Cyprus grasped it like a lifeline and, with a grunt, allowed Wallaig to pull him to his feet.

A gust of wind swirled into the LZ. The mountain groaned.

Cyprus swayed, fighting to maintain his balance. A big hand landed on his shoulder, steadying him. Swiping the blood from his brow, he met his first in command's damaged eyes. Scarred beyond repair, Wallaig's white pupils glowed in the gloom. The male stepped in close, pressing the points of his bloody knuckles into Cyprus's chest, right over his heart.

"Forgiven." Expression tight with regret, Wallaig touched his cheek to his, smearing Cyprus's blood on his skin. "You are a worthy male, Cyprus. Strong and honorable. I am proud to call you commander."

Standing in a semi-circle behind him, the other warriors murmured. Quiet voices all echoing the same sentiment—acceptance, absolution, the pride of calling him one of their own.

Relief rushed through him in a torrent of emotion. Cyprus shook as shock and disbelief collided. Tears pooled in his eyes. One fell, joining the blood on his cheek. Exhaling a shaky breath, he cleared his throat. Unbelievable. He hadn't dared hope. Had feared his warriors would reject him without hesitation after being told the truth, but...his chest tightened...the males he fought alongside understood instead, accepting his imperfection, forgiving him for his mistake, still comfortable under his command.

With a nod, Wallaig released him and stepped back.

One by one, his brothers-in-arms came forward. Each cupped his nape, thumped his chest and touched cheeks with him, the agony of hurting him a dark blight in their eyes. Their pain as great as the physical anguish now throbbing through his body.

The last in line, Tydrin approached on quiet feet. Tossing tradition aside, he didn't touch cheeks with him. His brother hugged him instead. "Well done, brother."

Returning the embrace, Cyprus rapped him on the back. "Thank you, Tydrin...you wee runt."

Tydrin laughed.

Wallaig snorted. "Enough with the love in. We've work to do tonight."

Grabbing Tydrin by the scruff of his neck, Wallaig yanked him away from Cyprus. As his brother stumbled backward, his first in command nailed him with a no-nonsense look. "What's the plan, lad?"

Rolling his shoulders, Cyprus met each warrior's gaze in turn. Mouthy Levin. Brutal Kruger. Stoic Rannock. Bad tempered Wallaig. And steadfast Tydrin. He flexed his fists, assuming the mantle of command as though it had never been in question.

"Now, we hunt," he said, sounding more beast than man as his dragon half took over. "Grizgunn wants my female. I pricked his pride when I took Elise from him. He'll search for any sign of her and—"

"You've fed from her?" Kruger asked, emerald green eyes intent on his face.

Cyprus nodded. "And fed her in return."

"Brilliant." Picking up a rock, Levin tossed the pebble from hand to hand. "You can mimic and broadcast her bio-energy like a signal. We'll set a trap, draw the bastards in and—"

Rannock growled. "Gut the arseholes, one at a fucking time."

"Exactly." Cyprus grinned, aches and pains forgotten as the thrill of the hunt coursed through him. "Pair up. Levin and Kruger, Wallaig and Rannock... Tydrin, you're with me. Everyone follow my lead."

Showing teeth, his warriors snarled in agreement.

Cyprus turned toward the ledge and, arms and legs pumping, ramped into a run. Footfalls hammering stone, he sprinted across the LZ. The toe of his boot meet the uneven edge. Without pause, he leapt into the void and, glorying in the blast of cold air, shifted into dragon form. His body lengthened. His hands and feet transformed into claws. Black and white orange-speckled scales replaced his human skin, spreading like wildfire as he unfolded his wings. An updraft lifted his bulk. Cyprus banked hard, rocketing between two jagged peaks. Brutality settling in his veins, he turned south toward Edinburgh. No time to waste. He had a rogue pack to hunt and Grizgunn to kill.

F laked out on her back, Elise woke in slow degrees. Her surroundings registered a little at a time. Comfortable mattress beneath her. Soft blankets wrapped around her. The scent of vanilla-infused candles floating in the air. As the smell drew her from the dreamscape, she shuffled on the cotton sheets and opened her eyes. She blinked, up and down: shift one leg, bend the other knee, wiggle her hips, and...

Sore muscles squawked in protest. A dull ache bloomed between her thighs.

Elise hummed in approval.

Oh, yeah. Cyprus and the luxurious feeling of post-orgasm delight. She sighed. He'd given her so many. Had made her come over and over. At first, she'd begged him for more. By the end, she'd been begging him to stop. Death by orgasm. Arching her back, Elise stretched out her arms and huffed. Who knew it was even possible? Not her. Not before yesterday. Women never complained about too much pleasure. And neither was she. Despite her aching muscles, the thought of Cyprus made her blood heat and need unfurl in her belly.

God. Something must be wrong with her.

She wanted him again.

Twisting onto her side, she scanned his side of the bed. Empty. No smoking hot guy lounging against the headboard waiting for her to wake up. Just a dented pillow and a tray covered by a fancy, embossed cover. A white piece of paper lay propped against the silver dome. Squinting, she forced her eyes to focus.

Mate,

EAT. You need your strength. I'll be back to see to you later.

LOVE,

Cyprus

ELISE GRINNED. Well, now. That almost sounded like a threat. A delicious, sexy one as she read between the lines, guessing his "seeing to her" would entail additional time in bed...and a lot more orgasms.

"You won't hear me complain."

With a short army crawl, she made it to the edge of the bed. Setting his note to one side, she plucked the lid off her breakfast. Or lunch. She pursed her lips. Could be dinner. Not that it mattered. Two croissants, a neat pile of wedged cheese, and...

"Fresh raspberries," she murmured, popping one into her mouth. A sweet tang exploded over her tongue. "Yum. My favorite."

The tiny taste made her stomach rumble for more. Wrapping the sheet under her arms, Elise pushed upright and, sitting cross-legged, grabbed a croissant. Hmm, French baked goods, flaky on the outside, soft on the inside, the perfect meal after mind-blowing sex with a gorgeous man. She took another bite and reached for the power drink Cyprus had left her.

A knock sounded on the door.

She opened her mouth to answer.

The door cracked open before she managed to say 'come in'. A redhead peeked through the narrow opening. "Are you decent?"

After last night? After all the depraved things Cyprus had done to her? Elise blinked. She wasn't sure *decent* was a word that applied to her anymore.

Setting her drink down, she leaned to one side. The shift improved her view of the intruder. Dark red hair surrounded a pretty face. Fair skin with freckles sprinkled across the bridge of her nose. Bright green eyes alight with mischief. "Ivy?"

"Hi." A small hand joined the face peering between the door and jamb. Fingers waved in greeting. Nails painted with purple sparkles winked at her in the candlelight. "Sorry, but I couldn't wait another second to meet you. You've been sleeping forever."

"Really?" Dying to meet Tydrin's mate, she waved Ivy into the room. "What time is it?"

"Almost midnight."

So late? Wow, she'd been out of it for hours. "God. Sorry. I just—"

Ivy snorted, cutting off her apology. "No worries. I didn't fare any better after my first night with Tydrin. Orgasm central. He nearly blew the top of my head off."

"I hear you," she murmured, feeling better about the fuzzy nature of her mental state. "I'm still a little muddled."

"Get used to it," Ivy said, wearing an impish grin.

"If Cyprus is anything like Tydrin, you're not going to be walking right for a while."

Elise laughed, liking Ivy already. Direct and to the point. Friendly with a wicked sense of humor. A woman she could relate to, a ready-made friend inside a lair full of dragon guys. Happiness bubbled up inside her. Strange, but there it was again—unabridged contentment, the sense she belonged here, that she'd finally found her place in the world.

Ripping off another piece of flaky goodness, she pointed to her plate. "Want a croissant?"

"Tempting, but...nah." After crossing the room, Ivy hopped onto her side of the bed. Leaning over, she surveyed Elise's plate and, after a second of indecision, stole a raspberry. "Tydrin left me breakfast before he took off."

"He's gone?"

"Cyprus, too."

The news hit her like a freight train at full speed. All her mental cars derailed, leaving her scrambling for a moment. Why? Elise frowned. The hell if she knew, but as distress streaked though her, she reached out with her mind, searching for Cyprus. For the elusive, yet powerful connection that tied her to him. Nothing. No zing in her veins. No echo of him inside her mind, just a coiled tether with an empty hook on one end and...no Cyprus.

Ivy wasn't lying. Cyprus wasn't in the lair.

Sucking in a breath, Elise struggled not to panic. Her reaction made no sense. She hardly knew him. Had spent all of two nights and one day with him, and yet somehow, he'd become vital to her. She felt his absence like an important manuscript missing from a prized collection. As though someone had stolen all the books off her shelves, leaving her without cover or context.

"Where did he go?" she asked, fighting to tamp down her unease.

"No need to panic, girlfriend." Understanding in her eyes, Ivy reached out. A warm hand settled over hers, steadying her, making her feel less crazy and more connected. "It takes time to adjust to the connection. Energy-fuse creates a powerful link between you and your mate. What you're feeling right now is completely normal."

"Normal? I feel as though I'm going to—"

"Explode? Go into meltdown?"

"Yes."

"Good." Ivy smiled, delight in her eyes. "It means the bond you share with Cyprus is not only strong, but active. It means I get a sister...and some freaking back-up."

Good? Was Ivy nuts? She didn't feel good...at all. Elise scowled at her new buddy. "What do you mean by *back-up*?"

"I'm the only girl here, and the guys are super protective. I feel as though I'm walking around in bubble wrap half the time." Gesturing with her hands, Ivy wiggled into a more comfortable position. "Like just last week, I wanted to visit Stirling—you know, to see William Wallace's broadsword?"

"Oh, my God," Elise murmured, nibbling on a piece of cheese. "I've always wanted to see that."

"I know, right?" Ivy threw her a look of long suffering. "Well, I happened to mention it to Levin in passing. He told Kruger, who told Wallaig. And that rat ran straight to Tydrin, so I got shut down. It wasn't as though I didn't plan to tell my mate, but...sheesh. The guys didn't give me a chance. They're worse than a room full of nannies."

"Annoying."

"You have no idea. Not yet anyway, but you will." Ivy grinned, the mischievous glint in her eyes a little disconcerting. "At least now, they'll have to split their attention between you and me. It'll totally distract them, which means I get more wiggle room."

"Oh, sure. Throw me under the bus, why don't you?"

"That's the plan."

Elise huffed in amusement. "Some friend you're turning out to be."

"Oh, you're awesome," Ivy said, laughing. "We're going to have so much fun together."

And get into a whole lot of trouble. Elise could see it now, Cyprus going all hard-faced when she refused to toe the line. "The guys are in for it now."

"Okay, good. We're on the same page." Looking delighted, Ivy rubbed her hands together. "Time to plan our first incursion, but first—get dressed. You look like you need coffee. Lord knows I do."

The suggestion made Elise groan. Coffee, her drug of choice.

Taking the sheet with her, Elise slipped off the bed. The second her feet hit the floor, she made for the bathroom. Her clothes were in there...somewhere. She remembered seeing her sweats on the floor while showering with Cyprus. Right before he drove her into a pleasure coma with his soapy fingers and tucked her into bed.

Hinges creaked as she pushed the door wide. Standing on the threshold, she scanned the space, looking for her clothes. Her brow furrowed. Not curled up in the corner beside the shower stall. Not under the cantilevered stone ledge full of fat candles throwing light into the room. Not jammed beneath the antique tub either. Elise turned full circle. Her gaze caught on the wooden vanity with multiple drawers and double sinks. Her heart clenched in appreciation. Folded neat as a pin on the granite countertop rested a pair of jeans, a dark tank-top, and a warm, zip-up hoodie. Cute lace-up running shoes sat beside the pile.

All in her size.

God bless Cyprus. He thought of everything.

Dressing in record time, she left the ensuite and—

"Ready?" Stealing another raspberry, Ivy raised a brow.

"Yup." Finger combing her hair, Elise skirted the foot of the bed. "Lead the way."

Five minutes, and some fast walking later, she walked under a familiar archway and followed Ivy into the great room. Halfway across, footfalls muffled by area rugs, she paused to look around. Same set up: couches, beanbag chairs, a kitchen kitted out with the best of everything. Her attention bounced from the old fashioned six burner stove to the enormous stainless steel refrigerator. Powered by magic, the appliance hummed, sending a quiet buzz into the air as light globes swayed overhead.

Lots of light. A comfortable space, but...quiet and empty.

No one around but her and Ivy.

Unease ghosted down her spine. Prickles shimmered over her nape, raising fine hairs, increasing her awareness. As her skin turned clammy, Elise looked around, instinct screaming for her to find safer ground, to run hard and hide fast. No rhyme. Zero reason.

Hugely paranoid, but the insistent thrum wouldn't die down or let go. It clutched at her instead, making her feel like prey, as though she was being hunted.

Standing beside the island, two mugs on the countertop and a carafe of coffee in her hand, Ivy glanced her way. She frowned. "What's wrong?"

Breathing too fast, Elise shook her head. "I don't know. Something's off and—"

Boom!

An explosion rocked the room. The walls trembled. The floor shook. Stone dust fell, coating her with filth as Ivy cursed and the carafe went flying.

Another tremor rumbled through the lair.

Elise stumbled sideways, knocking into an end table. Pain spiraled over her hip. The quaking increased, rolling into aftershocks as a familiar buzz burned between her temples. Oh God. She recognized the awful sinking sensation. Had felt it before in St. Giles Cathedral when...

"Ivy!" Her focus whipped back to her friend. On her ass, Ivy struggled to stand up. Fear giving her speed, Elise sprinted across the room, around the kitchen island, and hauled Ivy to her feet. "We need to get out of here. Right now."

"What's going on?"

"Griz—"

A roar blasted into the room. The sound of claws scraping over stone echoed up the tunnel.

Panic hit. Her heart slammed against the inside of her chest. "We need to hide. Where can we hide?"

"I don't know. Shit—I don't know." White-faced, Ivy clutched at her arm as Elise pulled her out of the kitchen. "I don't spend a lot of time here."

A dragon shrieked. More cacophonic roars. A

second later, the terrifying growls turned to words spoken by male voices.

"Oh, my God," Ivy whispered. "Whoever it is just shifted."

"Female!" Grizgunn's shout throbbed through the labyrinth. "I can smell you."

Her muscles tensed. Her mind raced. *A place to hide, a place to hide...*she needed a goddamn place to hide. Some place safe. Some place secure. Somewhere Grizgunn wouldn't be able to get in to and—

"The vault." Adrenaline hit her like rocket fuel. Dragging Ivy behind her, Elise sprinted across the great room. "Ivy—we need to get to the vault!"

"What vault?"

Elise didn't answer. She ran instead. Her shoes thumped up the stairs. The thud of heavy boots echoed across the great room. Heart pounding, Elise glanced over her shoulder. Standing in the doorway across the room, Grizgunn snarled as he spotted her.

"Come on, Ivy—run!"

Breathing down her neck, Ivy yelled, "I am—go!"

Running shoes providing grip, Elise raced across the vestibule, down the steps on the other side, and legs churning, skidded around the corner. Her knees skated across stone. Her palm slammed the dragon emblem in the center of the wood panel. The wall retreated to one side. Elise didn't wait for it to open all the way. She pressed her hand through the narrow opening. Her skin met steel.

"Open. Open. Please, open." Chest heaving, she pushed against the vault face. "Open Sesame!"

Magic hummed. A click sounded. The vault door started to open.

Grizgunn shouted at someone. "Get them!"

Afraid to look behind her, she shoved Ivy into the

wedge between steel jambs and followed her through. Her pant leg caught on metal. Grizgunn roared again. Gritting her teeth, she yanked at her leg. Denim ripped. Her foot cleared the doorway. Elise slammed her palms on the interior of vault, asking it to close, praying it listened before Grizgunn reached the library and pushed in behind her.

20

E yes on the sky, Cyprus leapt from his perch atop a high cliff. Cold air ruffled his wing-tips. Tucking each in tight, he landed on the church roof and climbed toward the steeple. His paws slipped across aging cooper. He curled his claws under. Metal groaned. The razor-sharp points of his talons bit, raking the hard surface, stopping his slid, making green flakes slough off and fall toward the cemetery below.

He hardly noticed.

The ancient tombstones snaking beneath tall trees didn't matter. Neither did the humans asleep in the small village less than a mile away. If all went well, none of the villagers would ever know he'd been here, on the outskirts of town, looking down over the snug hamlet they called home.

Tilting his head, he adjusted his sonar. Magic whispered through his veins. Tingles swept over his horns as he broadcast the signal. The invisible vibration went wide. He murmured in satisfaction. Mimicry at its best. Elise's bio-energy up and running, pulsing in concentric circles around him, surging through the air like a satellite signal. The perfect lure with which to set a trap. One Grizgunn would fly into any moment, except...

Cyprus frowned. The bastard should've arrived by now.

Firing up mind-speak, he nudged his first in command. *"Wallaig—anything?"*

Scales clicked, the sound impatient, accompanying a growl through the connection. *"Nary a peep."*

Not good. Wallaig's frustration signaled a trouble. The kind Cyprus refused ignore. Unflappable in a fight, uncanny at reading situations, his warrior was never wrong. Which meant if Wallaig didn't like the current of state of affairs, the plan he'd set in motion less than an hour ago was about to go sideways.

Swallowing a snarl, Cyprus touched base with the others. *"Anyone?"*

A round of 'nays' came through mind-speak.

Positioned outside the three-mile marker to avoid detection, his warriors waited alongside Wallaig. The plan was simple. Nothing fancy. Set a parameter, broadcast the signal, and wait for Grizgunn to take the bait. The instant the bastard flew into the kill zone, his pack would close ranks and unleash hell, annihilating the enemy in short order. A great strategy...if the bloody rogues ever bothered to show up.

Pushing from his crouch, Cyprus he wrapped his tail around his paws and searched the horizon. His brow furrowed. Nothing. No one. Not a single a ping on his radar.

Concern rattled the spikes along his spine. *"Something is wrong."*

"Agreed," Rannock said. *"It's taking too long."*

Levin grunted. *"With the strength of the signal, the rogues should've been here by now."*

"Which leaves us where?" Tydrin asked.

Good question. One he needed to answer—and fast—given Grizgunn didn't appear to be falling for the ploy. Any other dragon would have. His mate's bio-energy was powerful, irresistible to any male with a pulse and—

"*Fuck,*" Kruger said, sounding worried. "*We may be in trouble.*"

"*Tell me.*" Cyprus's tail twitched as his disquiet increased.

Kruger cracked his knuckles. "*Grizgunn is Randor's son. What if the bastard shared the location of the mountain lair before he died? What if—*"

Wallaig cursed. "*Grizgunn might know where we live.*"

"*Even if he does,*" Levin said. "*The protection spell will close ranks at the first sign of an intruder, shutting the doors in and out of the lair. Grizgunn won't be able to get inside.*"

"*Unless,*" Cyprus clenched his teeth as something horrible occurred to him. "*Randor was part of our pack. He lived in the lair before he fled. If Grizgunn's DNA is a close enough match tae his sire's, the shield might recognize him and—*"

"*Jesus,*" Tydrin said, panic in his voice. "*It'll let him walk right in. My mate—*"

"*Goddess, nay.*" Unfurling his wings, Cyprus took flight. He wheeled over the cemetery and banked north toward Cairngorm. He needed to return home... as fast as his wings could carry him. No time to waste. If Kruger was right, Grizgunn might already be inside the lair.

Terror tore at his heart. Elise. His mate. The female made and meant for him. If anything happened to her, he wouldn't survive. No matter how short their time together, Cyprus knew he couldn't live without her now. The bond he shared with her defied nature. Was so powerful the threads wrapped around his heart and squeezed, making him feel things he never had before.

Fear for her propelling him home, he reached out with his mind. If he could feel her, he could mind-speak with her. If he could warn her, then she might—

The bond flared, then sputtered and died.

He tried to link in again. Nothing came back. No signal. No connection. Just an empty void where energy-fuse should be, and a terrifying amount of silence.

head of the pack, Cyprus rocketed through a stone archway. Cairngorm and the mountain lair lay ahead. Less than five miles out, and... he was gaining fast. Flying in formation behind him, his warriors stayed on his tail, covering his six, searching for rogues hiding in ragged outcroppings. Snow whipped off high peaks and slate ledges, blasting over his scales, whipping into a squall, dialing visibility down to almost nothing.

Terrible conditions. Some might even say dangerous.

Squinting against the weather, Cyprus pushed himself hard and flew faster. No way would he slow down. He was close. Almost there. Just minutes away from landing on the LZ and—

His sonar pinged. The signal whiplashed, feeding him information, letting him know what lay ahead.

Cyprus bared the double row of his serrated teeth. *"Seven rogues on the east side."*

"I sense the bastards." Flipping up and over, Wallaig split wide right. Red scales flashed against white as wind whipped snow into a frenzy. *"Near the LZ."*

Tiger-striped navy, grey and gold scales blending

with the mountain side, Levin flew in, setting up off his left wing-tip. *"Is Grizgunn among them?"*

Recalibrating his magic, Cyprus searched for the male. *"Nay. No sign of him."*

His brother snarled. *"Goddamn it."*

"Steady, Tydrin," Rannock murmured, doing what he did best—staying calm when a situation went from bad to goat-fucked. *"You won't do Ivy any favors by losing your temper. If the arsehole's still here, he hasn't found our lasses yet."*

"Smart females," Kruger said, ice coating the long green spikes along his spine. *"They've found a place to hide."*

Trying to remain in control, so worried about Elise he couldn't join the conversation, Cyprus breathed in, breathed out, forcing himself to think. His warrior's words echoed inside his head. His brain stopped whirling for a second. He frowned. *A place to hide...a place to hide...a place to*—

"The vault," he rasped, relief releasing its grip on his throat. *"Bloody hell—the vault. They're in the vault."*

No wonder he couldn't feel her. Elise wasn't dead. She was in the fucking vault.

Designed to cage dragons when the Meridian re-aligned twice a year—now used to house the rare book library—the vault was protected by powerful magic. The kind able to lock a mature Dragonkind warrior inside when he became consumed by mating heat. A dangerous time for a male, which meant the vault boasted extra thick walls and a steel door that couldn't be broken. At least, from the inside. From the outside, though?

Worry hammered him. He didn't know. Had never tested—

"Will it hold?" Tydrin asked, plucking his concern out of thin air.

"Let's not find out." Wheeling around a corner, Cyprus set up his approach. *"We need tae get in there."*

"Fly around the other side, lads. Use the west entrance," Wallaig said. *"We'll hold the line, keep the bastards busy until you retrieve yer mates. Once yer free and clear, we'll peel off and make for the city lair."*

"Good enough." Cyprus nodded. Smart plan. Thank fuck for Wallaig. At least someone was thinking straight. Goddess knew it wasn't him right now. *"Tydrin...on my six."*

"Already there," Tydrin growled, banking hard, staying right behind him. *"Move your arse, brother. I need my mate."*

He didn't have to be told twice.

Splitting from the pack, Cyprus circled back and, flying low, jetted into a chasm. Long and deep, the fissure provided the right kind of cover. With Wallaig and the others providing a distraction, the enemy pack wouldn't see them, but—shite. The trench was narrow, so thin his wing-tips scraped over rock. Pain nipped at as hard friction burned his scales. He grimaced, but kept flying. Thirty seconds and he'd be out of range, completely invisible to the rogues under attack by the rest of his pack.

The west side of the mountain came into view.

Angling his head, he folded his wings and spiraled out of the ravine. Sheer rock face in front of him, narrow ledge above him. Body acting like a projectile, he rocketed straight up. At the last second, Cyprus unfurled his wings. The webbing caught air. His talons slid over rock and his claws dug in. Ripped from its mooring, granite shavings flew as he shot over the edge onto the ledge. Tucked into a somersault, he shifted from dragon to human form. Conjuring his clothes in mid-air, he tumbled across the platform.

One revolution. A second one and—

His boots slammed down. He legs took over, pumping as he sprinted across the LZ toward the door. He thumped on the portal with his mind, requesting safe passage as Tydrin landed behind him. Adding his request to Cyprus's, his brother hammered on the door.

Magic warped the air. Heat blasted over the landing, melting ice and snow. The stone wall disappeared, leaving behind an open archway.

Ducking his head to avoid the lintel, Cyprus crossed the threshold and ran to his right. Warm air blasted over him as the dark tunnel closed around him. His night vision sparked. Details came into focus: compact dirt floors and scorched walls marred by a recent fire, chisel marks covered in soot. A loud bang echoed through the lair. The sound of shouting followed. Slowing to a stop, Cyprus held his breath and listened. He needed to know how many warriors were inside the lair. The voices came again—frustration alive in each syllable.

He glanced over his shoulder. *"Three males."*

His brother nodded. A clang echoed through the labyrinth. *"With crowbars."*

Metal struck metal again. One strike turned into more, the high-pitched sound reverberating through the lair as Grizgunn tried to break into the vault.

Cyprus snarled. Thank the goddess for his mate's quick thinking. She made him so proud and...fuck. He could imagine her reaction: the realization his enemy had breached the lair, her fear as she ran for her life, the uncertainty as she locked herself inside the vault, hoping it would protect her. The scene played out like a bad movie inside his mind. Cyprus ground his teeth together. He couldn't wait to get his hands on Grizgunn. He'd rip his heart from his chest. He'd tear his head from his fucking shoulders for frightening his mate. Again. For the second time in as many days, but first...Elise.

Despite his desire for vengeance, she came before all else.

He must get her out of the vault, and then out of lair. No way would he be able to function in a fight unless he knew she was safe. The realization tempered his anger and slowed his pace. He needed the element of surprise. Wanted to surprise the bastards and make each warrior hesitate. Victory lived in that moment—in his ability to send another male running—so instead of rushing, he crept down the corridor, searching every jut in along the tunnel wall. He heard three males, but that didn't mean Grizgunn hadn't sprinkled more inside the lair. A good bet, given the Dane's success rate so far.

Coming to a fork in the passage, Cyprus veered left into a narrow hallway. Dirt turned to mosaic tiles beneath his feet. Light bloomed up head. The voices grew louder as the shimmer of globes against a vestibule ceiling came into view. The library, dead ahead: one left turn and a twenty second sprint away.

He flexed his hands. *"Get ready, brother."*

"Blitz attack?"

"Aye. I want them scrambling before they know what hit them."

"I'll hold the bastards at bay." Purple eyes aglow, Tydrin bared his teeth. *"You get into the vault."*

"Use whatever means necessary." Fueled by worry and rage, magic circled the center of his palms, itching

to be unleashed. *"Fists. Fire and acid. I donnae care if we burn the lair down, just as long as we get our mates out."*

"Agreed. Now—go."

Cyprus ran toward the vestibule. His feet churned over stone. Three steps straight ahead. He vaulted over the treads and, soles sliding over tile, pivoted toward the archway into the library. Three males holding crowbars looked up. Grizgunn's red-gold eyes met his and widened in surprise. The bastard sucked in a breath. Cyprus roared and unleashed hell. Fire burst from his palms, shooting out in a ribbon of orange flame. The magic-born whip snapped out, sailed wide, then came back around. The tongue lashed at the closest male.

Backpedaling, the rogue dropped his crowbar.

Metal banged against stone.

Cyprus didn't stop. He wrapped the lash around his enemy's leg. Fire and acid burned through clothes to incinerate skin and scorch bone. The male howled in pain, flailing, fighting to get free. Baring his teeth, Cyprus yanked him of his feet and conjured a second fire whip as Tydrin roared behind him. The battle cry blasted through the library. Heavy wooden shelves teetered. Books tumbled off shelves and hit the floor. Without losing speed, his brother ducked beneath the slashing fury of his fire whips and vaulted into the room.

"Retreat," Grizgunn yelled at his warriors, sprinting toward the rear of the room. "Move it! This way!"

Hurdling a couch, Tydrin gave chase.

With a flick, Cyprus held the third rogue immobile. The male rasped "mercy". He refused to show any. With a flick, he snapped the second whip around the arshole's neck and yanked. Fire and acid cut through skin and bone. His head left his shoulders. Expression blank, it bounced across the floor, coming to a stop next to the vault door before disintegrating into a pile of ash.

A crash sounded. A bookcase tipped over. Wood splintered, ripping through the stacks as a gust of fresh air blew into the library.

Out of view, Tydrin snarled, "Fucking hell. The bloody cowards. They entered a hidden tunnel."

"Donnae follow," he shouted, guessing Grizgunn had already escaped. Shite. The bastard was probably airborne, tail tucked between his legs, flying south to safety. "Stay with me, Tydrin."

His brother growled in answer.

Cyprus didn't wait a second longer to approach the vault. Dented in places, scorched by fire in others, the steel face looked battered. He slammed his palm against it. "Open."

Magic swirled in the air. Hinges groaned. The door began to open, widening slowly, making his heart thump and—

A piece of wood came hurtling out of the vault.

He dodged, diving to his left. The projectile sailed past, missing him by an inch, and slammed into the standing case behind him. Glass shattered. Relief made him huff. "You've got a good arm, lass."

A pause. A shuffling sound. "Cyprus?"

"Aye, *talmina*," he murmured, fingers flexing, wanting to get his hands on her, trying to be patient as the vault opened wider. "Come out of there. We need tae go."

Leaning to one side, Elise peeked between the door edge and the jamb. Tears pooled in her eyes as she spotted him. A second later, she dropped the table leg she held like a cricket bat and launched herself like a bullet through the opening.

Her target? Him.

With a murmur of relief, Cyprus closed his arms around her.

Burrowing into his embrace, she fisted her hands in the back of his shirt. "Thank God, thank God, thank God. I was so scared."

"Easy, baby. I've got you," he whispered, stroking his hands along her back, comforting her, reassuring himself. Scared, but alive. Trembling against him, but uninjured. "I've got you, Elise."

"Cy," Tydrin murmured, holding his mate, already halfway to the exit. "Time to move."

Loathe to let Elise go, but knowing he needed to, Cyprus took a deep breath and lifted his chin from the top of her head. His arms loosened around her. She clutched at him, refusing to release him. He didn't make her. Holding her tight, he picked her up and followed his brother out of the library—and out of the lair. He didn't look back. He didn't mourn the place he'd lived in all his life. And as he reached the LZ, shifted into dragon form and, cradling her close, leapt off the edge into the night sky, Cyprus didn't care that he would never return to it.

The lair was just a place. A shell, empty and cold without her in it. His mate was all that mattered. Elise was now his home, and he was never going to let her go.

D eep underground, standing in the library inside the city lair, Elise set her hands on her hips and looked around. Almost done. Another day or two, and the guys would finish installing the last bit of the molding. Dismantled and brought, piece by piece, from the mountain lair by Cyprus and his warriors, the new library looked very similar to the old—identical layout, same circular staircase rising to the second level and hand-carved bookshelves.

Perfect symmetry. Exceptional craftsmanship.

A lovely place, more work of art than study room.

At first, she'd worried, telling the guys not to bother. Given the recent attacks on the pack, returning to the mountain lair was dangerous. Elise shook her head. As beautiful at the library was, rebuilding it wasn't worth the risk. Or their lives. Grizgunn remained out there—somewhere—circling like a buzzard, hunting the Scottish pack, attacking when least...

Elise pursed her lips. Well, okay—not when least expected.

The warriors never got taken by surprise. Heck,

the crazy bunch wanted to be found. Made no attempt whatsoever to hide when they flew out of Aberdeen each night, relishing the opportunity to fight, wanting to right the wrong done to her and Ivy. Her lips curved. Beyond stubborn. So flipping loyal. The absolute best guys to have around. Proof positive lay in foundation of her new library—and all the books the warriors continued to deliver.

Elise glanced at the stacks littering the floor. And the new furniture Cyprus kept ordering. Bigger glass cases to house and protect important manuscripts. Two enormous worktables, sitting alongside a group of sturdy chairs. New couches and deep-seated armchairs (the last ones hadn't survived Cyprus's fire whip). She wrinkled her nose, the memory of burning cushions occupying her mind as she surveyed her favorite addition to the room.

A whole new section.

Feet doing a jig on the recently installed mosaic tiles, Elise stared at her workroom. Tucked beneath the second-floor walkway, the new addition matched the old décor, but had been built from scratch and stretched wall-to-wall, spanning the entire back of the room. Fronted by glass, the space belonged to her. A gift from Cyprus, complete with a worktable, book conservation tools, and a closed ventilation system with temperature control to keep old books in pristine condition. But her favorite? Elise grinned. The rare book collection transported from the mountain lair.

Everything a girl with a book fetish could want or need.

All in a very beautiful place.

Her heart gave a happy hop. God, she loved it here. Loved her mate. Adored her new family of dragon guys. Everything about her new life suited her, filling a hole inside she hadn't realized stood empty...until meeting Cyprus.

As if thinking about him conjured him, heavy footfalls sounded behind her. "Daydreaming again, are we?"

The timbre of his baritone sent shivers down her spine. Unable to contain her joy, Elise glanced over her shoulder and grinned. "It's almost finished."

His eyes crinkled at the corners. "It is at that, lass."

Setting down a box of books next to a stack of others, he approached on silent feet. His arms came around her from behind, hugging her close, making her wiggle in delight. Nipping the shell of her ear, he asked, "Happy?"

"Unbelievably." With a sigh, she leaned against his chest. His body heat warmed her, making her remember how good he always felt in bed. Hmm, silk sheets and Cyprus. Nothing better in the world than that, but...Elise cleared her throat. First things first. Time to get real and be honest. "I know I haven't told you yet, but..."

As her voice trailed off, he gave her a gentle squeeze. "What?"

Turning in his embrace, she set her hands on his chest and met his gaze. "I love you, Cyprus."

"*Talmina*." He drew in a soft breath. Fierce emotion sparked in his pale eyes. As his gaze started to glow, making her feel beautiful, he pressed his cheek to hers. "I love you too."

"I know," she whispered.

He'd been so brave, saying it first almost two weeks ago. Coming around—arriving here, being courageous enough to face this moment—had taken her more time. Not because she didn't love him. Elise had known right from the start how she felt about Cyprus.

She belonged to him. He belonged to her. No need to question or explore further. But it had all happened so fast, she'd needed time to adjust and think and...accept.

"Not because of all this." Waving her hand, she gestured to the library. "I mean, the book room is a beautiful gift and I'll cherish it always, but I want you to know I love you because of you. Because of who you are, not what you give me." Stroking her fingers along his jaw, she raised up on tiptoes and kissed him softly. "I belong here, Cyprus...with you."

"Aye, you do, lass," he murmured. "And I'll never let you go."

She smiled against his mouth. "Perfect."

And it was—*perfect*. Forever began and ended in his arms. She held happiness by the tip its tail, and had a future with a man who loved her more than she did books. Close the gilded cover. Happily-ever after guaranteed.

A NOTE FROM THE AUTHOR

Thank you for taking the time to read Fury of a High-land Dragon. If you enjoyed it, please help others find my books so they can enjoy them too.

Recommend it: Please help other readers find this book by recommending it to friends, readers' groups, and discussion boards.

Review it: Let other readers know what you liked or didn't like about Fury of a Highland Dragon.

Lend it: This e-book is lending-enabled, so feel free to share it with your friends. Sign up for my news-letter to receive new release information and other freebies. You can follow me on Facebook or on Twitter under @coreenecallahan.

Book updates can be found at www.CoreeneCalla-han.com

Thanks again for taking the time to read my books!

PREVIEW FURY OF DENIAL

1

EDINBURGH, SCOTLAND

The wind shifted, carrying the stink of city streets. The scent of garbage rotting in alleyways. The chemicals contaminating the water in half frozen gutters. The roll of smoke from fires burning in metal drums beneath highway overpasses. Even from his vantage point high in the sky, Wallaig smelled the putrefaction. The toxic swill rose to taunt him, painting a picture of a place in decline as clean air thickened into man-made smog.

Descending through the haze, he looked left to right. The urban landscape blazed like a multi-colored grid, creating a framework, allowing him to see in the dark.

Wallaig snorted. *See.* Seemed like the wrong word to use.

He couldn't *see* much of anything. His damaged retinas wouldn't let him. Not that he cared at the moment. With his dragon in full flight, his sightlessness didn't matter. Magic took the lead, drawing his particular talent to the foreground—the ability to sense energy in all things. Dead, alive, the object of interest didn't matter. If it existed—and held space in the world—he detected it before others of his kind knew it was there. A distinct advantage for any dragon warrior, but for him a necessity...and the only reason he'd flown out of the lair alone tonight.

Not the smartest move.

He could get into real trouble out here. On his own. In the dead of night one hundred and twenty miles from home with rogues in the area and no pack mates watching his six. But the honorable couldn't always be honest. Sometimes subterfuge walked hand-in-hand with doing the right thing.

Focused on a borough west of his position, he angled his wings and sliced through heavy cloud cover. Rimmed by blue, building tops came into view. Colorful energy streams converged, surrounding the neighbourhood like an iridescent rainbow, helping him distinguish animate from inanimate. A cluster of rats tucked beneath a row of dumpsters glowed yellow. The casement above their coiled tails pulsed a greyish-white. Street lamps went from dull pinpricks to glowing steel towers with dirty glass heads.

Wallaig grimaced. So much filth. Little to recommend. His nose twitched. His dragon half rebelled, urging him to turn around and fly home.

The need to heed the warning poked at him.

He hesitated mid-glide, then shook his head. Leaving a task undone wasn't an option. Not his usual MO either, so instead of copping out, Wallaig clung to his convictions and wings spread wide, aimed for the nearest rooftop. His back paws thumped down first. Blood-red scales rattled as his claws scraped along the parapet. Metal squawked a second before the beam dimpled beneath his weight. He flexed his talons, tightening his grip on the sagging roofline, and scanned the pixilated rise of tall structures against the dark horizon.

Wings tucked in tight, he crouched low and glanced over his shoulder. So far, so good. No rogues in pursuit. None of his brothers-in-arms giving chase. All in all, a good start to an already fucked up mission.

Shuffling sideways, he peered around a crumbling chimney top. He spotted the five-story walk-up three streets over. Brick facade, chipped stone trim, rusted balconies leaning in dangerous directions. Just as she'd described—a rundown shite hole in Edinburgh's west end, no need for guesswork.

With a grunt, he examined the building more closely. His gaze settled on the lone plastic chair close to the roof's edge. Huh, someone enjoyed being outside. A smoker, maybe. An idealist, perhaps, a human brave enough to sit out at night with huge dreams and even bigger plans. Dragging his gaze from the warped seat cushion, he focused on the entrance. Outlined in bright blue, the door led into the complex from the rooftop. His way in. One story down. A single staircase to navigate, a quick walk down a short corridor to leave the letters he carried on the counter in apartment seventeen.

No sweat. In and out in under five minutes. Six tops, if he took his time.

Wallaig hopped from his perch. His spiked tail lashed through cold air as he landed beside the chimney. The timbers supporting the roof groaned. Bricks cracked together, sprinkling him with stone dust, warning of an impending topple. Ignoring the threat of structural collapse, he picked his way across ancient asphalt tiles. Moss and clunks of tar peeled away, pushing between his toes as a garbage truck rumbled past on the street below. Snorting in distaste, he raised his paw to shake the debris from his claws. The black gunk stuck like barnacles to the bottom of a boat.

He curled his upper lip. Fucking disgusting and—

"Ah, hell," he grumbled, taking a closer look. "That shite's going tae stain."

Served him right. Fuck him and his soft heart. Or mayhap, the problem originated inside his idiot head. A complete lack of brain power explained a lot—like why he stood in the midst of a city he despised playing messenger for his commander's mate.

Ridiculous. His pre-dawn escapade qualified as bampot crazy. Particularly since sending a bloody email would've taken one-point-two seconds instead of the rest of his night.

But then, Elise had been persuasive.

Worried for her friend, she'd wanted to call and explain her sudden disappearance from Edinburgh. Cyprus kept telling his mate no, and Wallaig agreed with his commander's stance. Continued contact with the human world—and Elise's friend—wasn't a good idea. It was dangerous to both Elise and Dragonkind. As the newest member of the pack, Elise understood the need for secrecy, promising to cut all ties to her old life, ensuring the safety of all.

Logical argument. Sensible course of action. Nothing wrong with the dictate—other than the fact it was hurting a female he'd sworn to protect.

Wallaig shook his head. He should leave well enough alone. Ought to unfurl his wings and head for home. The balance inside the lair was good. Cyprus had claimed his mate. Elise adored him in return. Toss in the fact she loved her new life inside the Scottish pack and...absolutely. Zero question in his mind. He had no right to stick his nose in where it didn't belong. And yet, her upset didn't sit well with him.

He disliked the guilt he sensed in her. Hated that Elise believed she'd abandoned her friend. Pretty personal stuff, and something he shouldn't know. His fault from beginning to end. He never should have read the letters—the ones she wrote to make herself feel better about leaving Amantha behind without an explanation.

In his defence, he hadn't gone looking. He stumbled upon the correspondence by accident. Distracted by some new book in the library, Elise had left her letters unattended—and one half finished—in a wooden box in the middle of the coffee table. Open top. In plain view. Recipient made obvious by the 'Dear Amantha' scribbled across fancy paper. Curiosity forced his arse onto the couch. His dragon half had done the rest, helping him read the words, making each letter glow like pixels on a computer screen.

He swallowed a growl.

Goddess smite him dead with a thunder bolt.

He ought to be shot for invading her privacy. Cyprus certainly would after learning of his ill-advised trip tonight. He deserved whatever unpleasantness his commander threw his way. Another excellent reason to turn his arse around. The situation could be salvaged if he arrived home before dawn. No one would be the wiser and...

Wallaig clenched his teeth. Nay. Not going to happen. He hadn't flown this far only to back out now. He refused to abandon his plan. Elise needed closure. He could give it to her by playing errand lad tonight. So, best to get a move on. Standing around all night wasn't going to get the neat bundle of letters delivered on the sly.

Eyeing his target, he rechecked his sightline while attempting to shake the gunk off his paw one more time. No luck. Nothing budged. He was stuck with the shite—literally.

He exhaled in frustration. Lava shot from between his fangs and splashed across the rooftop. Exposed wood caught fire. Smoke swirled into a funnel fed by a ravenous orange glow. Mesmerized by the quick burn, he watched the flames grow into twin spirals before snuffing it out. Unleashing his flamethrower qualified as stupid. He might be a bit of a pyromaniac, but he refused to let the fire burn. The surrounding buildings couldn't take it. One misstep, and the whole block would burst into flames. Fun to watch. Not great to clean up. Too many humans would end up char-broiled.

Extinguishing the last ember, he leapt from one rooftop onto the next. On the third jump, he reached the building where the female lived. He landed with a soft thump. The plastic chair scuttled sideways, then tipped over, landing on a mound of dirt. Leftovers from a garden plot or...he sniffed the air...a pile of sheep dung? The second option seemed like a better guess given the stench and—

Bloody hell. What a pit.

Every time he flew south from Aberdeen, he re-membered why he never wanted to do it again. The building top he stood on wasn't changing his mind. Transforming from dragon to human form, he con-jured his clothes. A long-sleeved tee and his favorite jeans settled on his skin. He stomped his feet into his boots and started toward the door. Frigid wind gusts ruffled the hair at his nape. Ignoring the chill, he reached out and grabbed the handle. A quick yank. A shrill shriek of hinges. Wallaig stepped over the threshold and, footfalls banging across the landing, descended into the bowels of human society.

The smell of urine greeted him.

He wrinkled his nose. Hellfire in a hospital. What

in the god's name were human officials thinking? The odour alone screamed neglect. The rickety railing and crumbling concrete steps did the rest. No wonder Elise worried for her friend. The apartment complex should've been bulldozed decades ago. Rounding the fifth-floor landing, Wallaig stepped over a collection of used condoms. He grunted in disgust. Christ help him. Sex in a filthy stairwell. So classy...and not a place a female should be living alone.

Everything about the neighborhood screamed unsafe.

The state of disrepair backed up his theory.

Wallaig scowled. What was the female thinking? Why the hell was she living in such a shite hole? Serious questions in need of quick answers. Otherwise, he might do something stupid, like ditch the mission —along with the rules—and save Amantha from the building she lived in before the walls fell down around her.

Continue reading Fury of Denial. Buy it now.

ALSO BY COREENE CALLAHAN

Dragonfury Scotland
Fury of a Highland Dragon
Fury of Shadows
Fury of Denial
Fury of Persuasion

Dragonfury Short Story Collection
Fury of Fate
Fury of Conviction

Dragonfury Series
Fury of Fire
Fury of Ice
Fury of Seduction
Fury of Desire
Fury of Obsession
Fury of Surrender

Circle of Seven Series
Knight Awakened
Knight Avenged

Warriors of the Realm Series
Warrior's Revenge

ABOUT THE AUTHOR

 Coreene Callahan is the bestselling author of the Dragonfury Novels and Circle of Seven Series, in which she combines her love of romance and adventure with her passion for history. After graduating with honors in psychology and taking a detour to work in interior design, Coreene finally returned to her first love: writing. Her debut novel, *Fury of Fire* was a finalist in the New Jersey Romance Writers Golden Leaf Contest in two categories: Best First Book and Best Paranormal. She lives in Canada with her family, a spirited Anatolian Shepard, and her wild imaginary world.